Tales from Silver Lands

TALES
FROM
SILVER LANDS

Charles J. Finger

Woodcuts by Paul Honoré

Doubleday

NEW YORK   LONDON   TORONTO   SYDNEY   AUCKLAND

Published by Doubleday, a division of
Bantam Doubleday Dell Publishing Group, Inc.
666 Fifth Avenue, New York, New York 10103

Doubleday and the portrayal of an anchor with a
dolphin are trademarks of Doubleday, a division of
Bantam Doubleday Dell Publishing Group, Inc.

ISBN 0-385-07513-8
Copyright 1924, by
Doubleday, a division of
Bantam Doubleday Dell Publishing Group, Inc.
All Rights Reserved
Printed in the United States of America

16 18 20 19 17 15

BG

TO THE GOLDEN HEARTED
Carl Sandburg
AND HIS FRIENDS, MY CHILDREN
Helen and Herbert

CONTENTS

WOODCUTS

A TALE OF THREE TAILS

DOWN in Honduras there is a town called Pueblo de Chamelecón which is not much of a town after all. There is only one street in it, and the houses are like big beehives that have been squared up, and the roofs are of straw. There is no sidewalk, no roadway, and the houses are unfenced, so that you step from the room into the sandy street and, because of the heat, when you are inside you wish that you were out, and when you are outside you wish that you were in. So the children of the place spend much time down at the little river. At least they did when I was there.

I rode there on a donkey and, the day being hot, let the animal graze, or sleep, or think, or dream, or work out problems—or whatever it is that a donkey does with his spare time—and I watched the children in the water. There was one, a little baby just able to toddle around, who crawled down to the water's edge, rolled in and swam about like a little dog, much as the babies of Tierra del Fuego will swim in the icy waters of the Far South. He came out on my side of the water, as lively as a grig, smiling every bit as friendly as any other little chap of his age, white, brown, or yellow.

I stayed there that night because the day did not get cool and in the evening the people sat outside of their houses and played the guitar and sang. Now I had with me a little musical instrument like a tiny organ, which I bought in France, and it was so compact and handy that I could carry it everywhere as easily as I could a blanket. In fact, I used to ride with it behind my saddle, wrapped in my bedding. Well, as the people seemed to like their music, I brought out mine, so we had a very jolly concert, in spite of my poor voice, which they politely pretended not to notice. Then later, from curiosity, the children came about me and, to amuse them as well as myself, having done so badly at the singing, I did a few tricks with wads of rolled paper and a couple of tin cups, and the little boy who had swum across the pond laughed as loudly as any one there. That pleased his father mightily, so much indeed that he brought me a cup of goat's milk and some cassava bread and told me that I was a fine fellow. To please me further, he sang a very, very long song. It was all about the parrot and the wonderful things it did, a parrot that had lived long among people and learned their songs, and when the bird flew back to the forest, it still sang, and so well that all the other parrots in the forest learned to sing the song from beginning to end. But what was curious was that at the end of every other verse, there was this line:

When the rat had a tail like a horse.

So when he had done I asked him about that, for all the rats I had seen had tails which were far from beautiful, according to my notion.

The man listened gravely, then said: "But certainly, once the rat had a tail like a horse."

"When was that?" I asked.

"When the rabbit had a tail like a cat," he said.

"But I am still puzzled," I told him. "Was it long ago?"

"It was when the deer's tail was plumed like the tail of a dog," he told me.

As we talked, a kind of polite silence was upon all the people gathered about us; then a very, very old woman who was smoking a cigar nodded her head and said: "But Tio Ravenna is right. It was in the days of Hunbatz, who lived on beetles and spiders, and I heard it from my mother's mother, and she from the mother of her mother." Then the old woman went on smoking with her eyes closed, and all who were there nodded at one another, thinking, I suppose, that the old grandmother would presently tell the story. But of course, they who knew her well were wiser than to ask her to tell the Tale of Three Tails, so every one waited.

Presently, a little girl gave the old grandmother a piece of sugar and asked: "Was it two brothers, or three, who had to clear the great forest? I am not sure."

At that the little old lady's eyes were bright and she threw away her cigar and said:

"Two brothers. That I have told you before." After a little sigh, which was only pretending that she was weary of telling the tale, she said: "You know that I have told it to you before, and it is wrong that I should have to tell it so often. But you see this."

So saying, she took from her bosom, where she had it fastened to a silk thread, a little piece of jade and let us see it. It was broken from a larger piece, but we could make out on it a carving which I saw to be a deer with a tail like a sheep dog's. We passed it about and every one looked at it carefully, although certainly all of them must have seen it time and time again, and when it came to the old grandmother again she replaced it and told us the Tale of Three Tails, just as I have written it here.

Once, long ago, the rat had a beautiful tail like a horse, with long sweeping hairs, though it was before my time of life. It was in the days of old Hunbatz, and he was a wizard who lived in the dark of the great forest that used to be on the other side of the big river. In those days things were not as now and animals were different; some larger, some smaller. The deer, as you have seen on the stone I showed you, had a tail like a dog, and the rabbit's tail was long and furry like the tail of a cat.

Now in that land there was a hunter with whom neither lasso nor arrow ever failed, and he had two sons, beautiful to look at and brave of heart, stout and quick of foot. Not only did the brothers work better than any men had ever worked, but they could play ball and sing, throwing the ball higher than birds could fly, and singing in a way that brought the wild things to hear them. Nor was there living creature able to run as swiftly as the two brothers. The birds alone could outrace them.

The brothers being grown, their father thought that it was time for them to make a home for themselves, so chose a place on the farther side of the forest, and told them to clear it, which, he said, could be done in seven days. It was no little forest, you must remember, but a vast place, where sunlight never pierced, and the roots of trees were like great ropes; a jungle that stretched for miles and miles and the tangle in it was so thick that a monkey could barely get through without squeezing. Deep in the forest there was a blackness like the blackness of night. The trunks of the trees were so large that three men holding hands could not circle them and where there were no trees, there were vines and snakelike lianas and thorn bushes and flowers so great that a man could lie down to sleep in the shade of them.

The first day the brothers took a great space, piling the trees at one corner, clearing the tangle and leaving all as smooth as the water of a lake. They sang as they worked, and they sang as they rested in the heat of the day, and the organ bird and the flute bird answered them from the gold-green shade. So pleasant was their music that the old iguana, though he was as big as a man, came from his resting place in the trees to listen.

Seeing how things were going, old Hunbatz in the dark of the forest grew very angry, fearing that his hiding place would soon dwindle and vanish. So he went to the great gray owl, his friend, and they talked the matter over between them. The owl told Hunbatz that he must set the father's heart against the brothers, telling him that the boys were lazy and instead of working spent their time in playing with the ball and in singing.

"Go," said the owl, "to their father, and when he asks how the lads fare with their work, say to him:

> They sing and they play
> For half of the day.

It may fall out that he will grow angry and cut off their heads, and thus the forest will be safe for us."

That seemed to the wizard to be good advice, and before the close of the day's work, old Hunbatz, who could fly by flapping his hands in a certain way like a swimmer, cast

himself into the air and flew with great swiftness to the place
where the father lived. But he took care to dress himself like
a woodman.

"Well met," said the father, seeing Hunbatz, but thinking
him no wizard of course. "From where do you come?"

"From the other side of the forest," was the reply.

"Then perchance you saw my two sons who are clearing
the forest," said the father.

"I did," said Hunbatz.

"And how are the boys doing?" asked the father.

At that old Hunbatz shook his head sadly and answered,
as the owl had told him:

> "They sing and they play
> For half of the day."

That, you know, was quite untrue, for while they sang,
there was no stopping of work, and as for the play, it is true
that they threw the ball from one to the other, but so clever
were they that one would throw the ball so high that it would
take hours and hours before it came down again, and of
course, while it was in the air, the brothers went on working.

"I would cut off their heads to teach them a lesson," said
Hunbatz, "if they were sons of mine." Then he turned on
his heel and went away, not flying until he was out of the
father's sight, for he did not wish any man to know that he
was a wizard.

To be sure, the good man was grieved and his face
clouded, when he heard the tale of Hunbatz, but he said
nothing, and, a short time after, the brothers came home.
He was much surprised when, asking the lads how much
work they had done that day, they told him that they had

cleared off the space of forest he had bidden them to. After much thought he told them that the next day they would have to do twice as much as before. The brothers thought the new task hard, but they went to work with a good will and on the second day the trees fell like corn before a man with a machete, and before night they had finished that which they had been given to do.

Again old Hunbatz flew through the air to the father and tried to set him against the boys, and again that night, when the boys were home, their task was set for the next day twice as much as the day before.

It was the same the third day, and the fourth, until at last the boys came to a point where by the mightiest working they could not move a stick or a blade of grass more. And yet, because of old Hunbatz, the father set them a task still greater.

On the fifth day things looked very hopeless for the boys, and their hearts were sad as they looked at the forest and saw the task that their father had set them to do. They went to work feeling for the first time it would be impossible for the sun to go down on their finished task, and the heart of old Hunbatz was glad. But the birds in the forest were silent that morning, for they too knew that there were sad hearts in the brothers. Even the grasshoppers and the mosquitoes and the bees were still, and as for the boys, not a note of joy could they raise.

Then to them came the iguana, wise old lizard who knew everything that went on in the forest, and as soon as he had heard what the brothers had to say he smiled and called on them to listen, after making sure that there was no living creature to hear except the birds, for of them he had no fear, knowing that the birds tell no secrets.

"Be cheerful," said the iguana, "and I will tell you a charm. It is this: mark about the handles of your working tools rings of black, white, red, and green, and before you start to work, sing:

> I must do what I can,
> Is the thought of a man,

and if your hearts are brave, you will see what happens."

Having said this and smiled on the brothers, the old iguana climbed into a tree and stretched himself along the branch of it where he could best see, and the birds gathered in a great circle, a matchless melody going up to the sky.

So the brothers took their axes, their spades, their hoes, and their machetes, and painted about the handles of them rings of black and of white and of red and of green, and their voices rang sweet and clear as they sang, as the iguana had told them:

> "I must do what I can,
> Is the thought of a man."

No sooner had the last words passed than the whole company of birds broke out into a chorus, singing, chattering, chirping, whistling, screaming, each according to its manner and, without hands touching them, axes went to work cutting down trees, machetes chopped at lianas and vines, spades cleared and dug; and trees, bushes, and weeds piled themselves in great heaps at the edge of the clearing, so that in less than an hour the whole task was done. Then it was that all things in the forest were glad and the good iguana smiled broadly. The very monkeys joined in and, catching the ball which the brothers threw, tossed it from tree to tree until it passed through the whole jungle and back again.

But old Hunbatz was angry beyond measure, so angry that he whirled about on his heels three hundred times, turning so rapidly that he looked like a storm cloud, and his long whiskers were tangled about him like a mantle. But the faster he whirled, the more his anger boiled, and, flapping his hands, he shot into the air, going so swiftly that his very clothes were scorched.

"How are the boys?" asked the father, when Hunbatz stood before him.

For answer, Hunbatz screamed: "Your boys are idle fellows!

> "They sing and they play
> For half of the day."

Had I such sons, I would cut their heads off to teach them a lesson."

Said the father: "To-morrow I shall go to the forest, and if you have not spoken truth, then this arrow which has never yet missed a mark shall find one in your heart. But if it is as you say, then my sons shall feel my anger."

Old Hunbatz did not like that at all, for well he knew that the hunter's arrows were never wasted. So back he flew to the owl and the two of them whispered together. That night there was a great gathering of the animals: of the hare, the deer, the rat, the jaguar, the puma, the opossum, and many others. The rat, the deer, and the rabbit led them, and in a wonderfully short time, not only were all things restored and the work of the day undone, but the trees and the bushes and the vines and the lianas that had been moved on the other days were put back in their old places, growing and blooming, so that all was as though the brothers had never been at the forest at all.

Sad was the hour the next morning when the hunter came
with his two sons and saw the forest as though hand had
never touched it. The brothers could not believe their eyes.
Grinning from the thick of a rubber tree was the face of
Hunbatz, and on his shoulder was the owl. For a moment
the father thought to cut off the heads of the lads to teach
them a lesson, but on second thought he told them that he
would give them another chance.

"What should have been done is not done," he said. "I
will grant you a day and a night to clear all the forest as
you told me it was cleared. To-morrow morning I will come
again, and see whether all is well done." At that he left them
and went his way.

No sooner had he gone than the two brothers went to see
the iguana, who told them of the witchery of the owl and
Hunbatz and bade them to act as before. So they made the
ring about the handles of their working tools once more and
sang:

"I must do what I can,
Is the thought of a man,"

and, as on the day before, axes, machetes, and spades went
to work and in a short time all was clear again. Then the
iguana told the brothers of the evil that Hunbatz had done
and bade them set traps and keep watch that night. So three
traps were made and set, and when night fell, from all parts
of the forest there came animals led by the rat, the deer, and
the rabbit, and old Hunbatz and the owl watched from the
dark caves of the leaves.

No sooner had the first three animals stepped into the
clearing than they were caught fast in the traps, whereupon
the rest of the animals turned and fled. Then the brothers

rushed to the traps. The rabbit gave a great jump when he felt the jaws close upon his beautiful catlike tail, but it was chopped off close to the body. The deer, with his tail like a plume, fared no better. So both deer and rabbit fled to the woods ashamed, and, as you see for yourself, have had no tails ever since. As for the rat, he was far too wise to jump as the rabbit and deer had done. But seeing the brothers coming, he pulled and pulled and pulled so that all the beautiful hair was stripped, leaving him with but a bare and ugly thing of a tail as you see to-day.

The next morning when the hunter-father came, there was the forest cleared and all in good order as the boys had said. So he sought out old Hunbatz, who flapped his hands and flew for very fear. But so fast he went that his clothes were burnt off, and his skin was baked into a hard crust by the great heat, and he fell to the earth and so became what we call an armadillo. As for the two brothers, they lived very happily for many, many years, and things went well with them and the land they lived in was a land of good harvest and fruit trees.

So now you know the Tale of Three Tails and if you do not believe it, look at the rat and the deer and the rabbit and the armadillo, and see for yourself.

THE MAGIC DOG

DOWN where the forest is so thick that the sun rarely pierces the leafy roof, where there are mosses and ferns and little plants of the brightest green, where parrots screech and thousands of little monkeys chatter in the trees, there stands a great white temple. Once, long ago, there was joy and gladness there, and flower-crowned people danced and sang, but now vines hang about the doors and window holes and there are tall rank weeds in the courtyard. Still, it is even now very beautiful, though sad to see.

Long years before this temple was built, there lived a king, and his people loved him, and he on his part loved not only his people, but every flower that grew, every grass blade and every leaf on bush and tree. Where he came from, none knew, but there were those who said that he had come from the sea, not in a ship with men, but alone, in a great and beautiful sea-shell. So they called him, in their own tongue, The King Who Came in a Sea-shell. And when he went about among his people he wore a headdress of gold-green feathers, a feather cloak of turquoise blue, and about his middle was a golden belt set with glittering precious stones. On his feet were golden sandals and in his hand he bore a great spear of silver. The spear he carried for a sign only, for there was no fighting in those days, and it was a time when all went very well. Every one had enough to eat and to drink and to wear, so that none had to worry about the day to come. Men loved diamonds and emeralds and rubies for their beauty, and just as they loved the sight of the tiny rainbow in a sparkling dew drop. As for other things, corn grew so large that a single ear was as much as a man could carry and cotton grew not only white, as we see it now, but red and blue and yellow and scarlet and black and orange and violet and green.

It was the daughter of the Sea-shell King who had taught the people how to grow coloured cotton, and she, with her silky cloud of hair, was the most beautiful creature ever seen. When she walked about, the air was sweet with wonderful perfume, birds sang with joy as though their throats would burst, and slim drooping ferns nodded a welcome.

The story of the beauty and goodness of the maiden ran through all the land, and young men who sought her hand came from far and wide. So many were her suitors that a day was set apart each week, when all the people gathered to see the young men display their powers or their gifts or their clevernesses. Some would shoot with the bow and others cast the lasso. Singers sang the songs they had made and musicians played their flutes so well that the slender boughs bent to listen. There were gifts, too, and some brought rare stones cut into the shapes of birds and animals and flowers, but not one man had touched the heart of the princess, though she was gracious to all.

Now before the king came, an evil creature of a witch

had ruled the land, and she had come from the Land of the Shaking Mud. Somehow, the Sea-shell King had driven her away and, that she should worry his people no more, he had set a boundary, and guards were on watch day and night to prevent her in her mischief. So she spent the day in her cave, coming out only at night to prowl about the boundary, and then only when there was no moon. Her name was Tlapa.

One day there came to the king a man in rags, who said that his name was Maconahola, and the king was glad to see him, the more so because age was creeping upon the king, and he sought someone wise and brave enough to rule in his place. But no sooner had the princess looked at the stranger than she cast down her eyes, saying that he had the face of the man she had seen in a dream. When the king asked her questions, she said that in her dream she had followed the stranger about, had slept at his feet, had tended his fields and made his clothes. At that her father was greatly astonished, for that his daughter should be the servant of a man who came clad in rags seemed strange indeed.

The second day, Maconahola was asked if he bore gifts, but he showed his empty hands. Then, to the end that no idle or useless man should be in that land, a time was set and Maconahola was ordered to appear before the young men and compete with them. At the test Maconahola stood very well. When the best bowman sent his arrow into the exact centre of the mark, Maconahola drew his bow and aimed so carefully that his arrow split the arrow of the other man. Nor was he less skilful with the lasso, casting his loop so that it fell about the smallest thing aimed at. It was much the same when the swiftest runner was brought. To be sure, he ran like a deer, but Maconahola ran like the wind, leaving

him far behind. As for the singing contest, when the stranger
sang the very birds were hushed and, the song being finished,
a great quetzal with jet-black wings, a scarlet breast, and head
and back of gold-green feathers, flew down and sat on the
shoulder of Maconahola.

Then a great shout went up, and all the bowmen, the lasso
throwers, the runners, and the singers came forward and
greeted Maconahola, for there was no jealousy in that land,
nor was there envy, and each had it in his mind to strive
for that which seemed best, caring nothing for self-advance-
ment. As for the king, being very old and tired, he was glad
indeed to find a man who might become ruler in his place.
So he stepped down from his high place and cast his coat
made of a thousand turquoise feathers about the stranger's
shoulders. All went very well indeed, and the princess was
happy to have found the man of her dreams, and the two
of them loved all things, so that all things embraced and
loved them.

But Tlapa, the witch with long crooked nails and black
teeth and ice-like eyes, learned of all this from the bats. Loving evil, and war, and violence, she was angry that another
should come into the land to rule when the old king died,
for she had long waited for the breath to pass from his body
so that she might rule again. Seeing how the people greeted
Maconahola, she became tight-lipped and slit-eyed. One
night she went to Roraima, a place of rocks, where lived a
wild man of terrible strength who sat in his cave all day,
crouched over a fire of smoking green wood. Over the cave
fire Tlapa and the wild man whispered long and long, while
bats flapped and fluttered and white worms crawled close to
listen, for they plotted how to dispose of Maconahola. The
wild man was all for dashing into the country, trampling

down the guards that stood in his way, and beating the stranger with his great club of long, blunt thorns. But that Tlapa would not hear of, knowing that Maconahola could shoot an arrow that would speedily put an end to the wild man of the rocks. Far more crafty was she, remembering and telling the wild man of a strange plant that grew in the gloomy depths of a forest far away, where, because of the tangled thicket, she could never go.

No sooner had the wild man learnt of the strange plant than he sprang to his feet and with great bounds went crashing through the forest, overturning trees that stood in his way, upsetting huge rocks, splashing through swamps, and climbing a rocky precipice like a wild cat until he came to the place where grew the evil weed. He was back again in his cave before midnight. Taking the weed, Tlapa dried it over a fire of rotten wood and crushed it into powder. The powder she cast into the air and, carried by the wind, it fell where the king's people lived. Wherever it fell, wherever it touched, there grew hate and suspicion, jealousy and greed. Where the dust fell on plant or flower, though there was but the slightest fleck of it, there was immediately a withering and a dying; the very corn shrivelled and shrunk. Where had been flowers, there grew in a single night dense, thorny tangle. The very weather changed and the pleasant cool passed away, so that the days were hot and the nights icy cold. Some men, touched with a strange greed, laid claim to great tracts of earth, bidding others begone, and so for the first time in that land men quarrelled and fought. Even the old king changed a little and, seeing the trouble that had come upon his land, was persuaded to believe that Maconahola was the cause.

Word passed from mouth to mouth and whispering tongues

poisoned truth, and when Maconahola took his walks, griev-
ing to see the withered flowers and fruits, people hid from
his gaze. Thoughts passed to words and words to deeds, and
one day a crowd turned on Maconahola and with sticks and
stones drove him across the border and into a forest where,
except for the cry of a distant bird, it was still as midnight.

Sad at heart, Maconahola built a little shelter of branches
and leaves and day after day wandered alone. Nor had he
living company until one day there came to him a dog, foot-
sore and thin. The creature was hungry and weak and thorn-
torn, and Maconahola took it in, washed and tended it, and
shared with it his meal. And a poor enough meal it was,
being of small berries and drops of tree gum and little roots.

In the morning when he went down to the stream to bathe,
the dog did not follow him, and on his return, to his vast
astonishment, he found in front of his house a field with
growing corn and many food plants. It had grown up in less
than an hour. So that evening he was full of gladness, and
with his dog walked about in full enjoyment of the beautiful
green earth, thankful for the humming bees and the gentle
wind that moved the leaves, thankful for the only living creature that was with him.

On the next day when he returned from his stream, having left the dog sleeping in the sun, he found that his little
bower of branches and leaves had been transformed to a
house with furnishings all simple, clean, and bright. And
around it were glorious flowers and fruits, and in the trees
birds sang, and humming birds, looking like flashing emeralds, darted through the leaves. So again his heart was full
of joy and thankfulness.

The third day he made as if to go to the river, but instead turned and hid himself behind the house to watch.

Then he saw the wonder, for the dog threw off its skin and there stood the beautiful maiden whom he had known as the king's daughter. At once she set about making garments of coloured cotton for him, and so rapidly she wrought that they fell from her hands like flower petals. Then she busied herself weaving a hammock of silk grass.

Maconahola made no sign, but went down to the river as usual and when he returned the dog ran to meet him, thrusting its moist nose into his hand. But the next day again he hid, and again the dog cast off its skin and the princess went to the garden, and to her came a cloud of humming birds. Swiftly Maconahola ran to the dogskin, picked it up and threw it into the fire, where it burned like dry leaves. Then the princess saw what had been done and gave a great cry of joy for the spell was broken; and Maconahola knew a fresh vigour of soul.

Hand in hand, they returned to the land, and the old king seeing them coming went out to meet them. And all the people were with him, overjoyed that Maconahola had returned, seeing the evil that had come upon them had not been removed with his departure. Overjoyed, too, were they to see the princess again, for none knew to what place she had gone, knowing only that she had vanished one evening, and at the same time a dog had run swiftly through their midst. For certainly, Tlapa the witch had laid some enchantment upon her with evil design. But evil, though it may touch the good, cannot for ever bind it, wherefore the maiden resumed her own form some part of every day.

There was a great meeting of all the people then, and Maconahola lost no time in seeking out the witch Tlapa, whom he killed with a silver pointed arrow shot through her heart. As for the wild man of Roraima, it is said that learning of the death of the witch, he dashed away in great terror and, sinking in the Shaking Mud, was seen no more. But the King of the Sea-shell made Maconahola a ruler, and on the spot where the bower had been built and where he first saw the dog there was erected the temple of white stone which you may see for yourself to this day if you go to Orinoco.

THE CALABASH MAN

THERE was once a woman who had an only son, and they lived in great contentment in a little house by the side of the lake and at the foot of a mountain. If you go to Guiana, you may see both lake and mountain to this day.

In all that land there was no lad so straight, so tall, so graceful as Aura, and, what is better still, he was kind and gentle. At the close of the day when he came from his fishing, he and his mother would sit in the cool of the evening, watching the glory of the sunset and listening to the music of the silver cascade which fell from the mountain into the lake. Often the forest animals would come and play about before their house. The lively little agouti would sport with the black jaguar and the great armadillo would let the coral snake coil on his shell, while birds of wondrous beauty flashed through the leaves of the trees like living fire. Great butterflies with silky white and green wings fluttered about the flowers showing their beauty, and from them the old mother learned the way to weave bright designs into the hammocks that she made of silk grass. At such times, before the sun dropped into its purple bed of cloud, and before the million glowworms lit their lights, the queen ant would sing:

> "From forest and hill
> We come at your will.
> Call, Aura, call!"

All went very well until one day Aura, going to the lake, found his basket net broken and torn, and taking it from the water saw with surprise that the fish which had been in it were eaten. Such a thing had never happened before, for in forest and hill he knew no enemy. As he stood in wonderment, the torn basket in his hand, he heard a voice behind him say:

> "From forest and hill
> We come at your will.
> Call, Aura, call!"

Looking around he saw a woodpecker, and the bright beady eyes of the bird were looking at him. Thereupon, Aura told the woodpecker to watch well, and setting a new basket net in the water he went a little way into the forest to gather wild fruits. Not far had he gone when he heard the watching woodpecker call, "Toc, Toc!" Swiftly he ran, but though he sped like a deer he was too late, for the second basket net was destroyed even more completely than the first and again the fish were devoured.

A third net was set, and this time he called upon the cuckoo to watch while he gathered his fruits. Very soon he heard the "Pon, pon!" of his new watcher and Aura lost no time in running to the lakeside. There in the water and close to the basket net was the flat, mud-coloured head of a swamp alligator with its dull and heavy-lidded eyes. Quick as lightning, Aura fitted an arrow to his bow and let fly, and the shaft struck the reptile between the eyes. A moment later the beast disappeared into the water.

The basket net had been partly broken by the alligator, but Aura mended it and again entered the forest. But before long he heard the cuckoo call, and much louder this time, so he ran like the wind, fitting an arrow to his bow as he went. On the lake-bank stood a beautiful Indian maiden in a gown that looked like silver, and she was weeping bitterly. At that Aura's heart was touched with pity, for he could see no living thing unhappy and remain happy himself. Gently he took her by the hand and asked her to tell him her name.

"Anu-Anaitu," she said, and smiled through her tears like the sun after a summer rain.

"From where do you come?" was his next question.

"Far, far away, where the great owl lives," she made reply, and pointed in the direction of the dark forest.

"And who is your father?" he asked, and at that there was a ripple of water rings on the lake and Aura thought he saw the nose of the alligator.

But she made no answer to his question. Instead, she covered her face with her hands and bent her head, so that her hair fell about her like a cloud.

Seeing her strange grief Aura said no more, but led her to his mother who received her kindly, and for many months the three of them dwelt together very happily. Yet whenever Anaitu thought of her father, she wept bitterly.

At last there came a day when Aura asked the maiden to be his wife and told her that if she would give him her hand, the two of them would make a journey to her own land so that she might say farewell to her people, telling them that she had made her home in a land of peace and brightness with those who loved her. Hearing that, little Anaitu wept with terror, telling Aura of the fearful journey that would be theirs, through a place where were great bats and gray hairy spiders and centipedes, and harmful and fearful things.

"Then stay with my mother and I shall go alone," said Aura, seeing her fear. "And I will seek out your father and tell him that all is well with you."

"That is worse still," cried the maiden, "for there is an evil spirit in my land and my father is bewitched. Seeing you, he will destroy you and your mother and me as well, once he learns where we are."

Greatly puzzled with all this, Aura went to see a wise old hermit who lived at the end of the lake, and to him he told his troubles and fears. After much thought, the hermit told Aura that he would make his journey in safety if he feared not and carried himself like a man. "And," said he, "if it should come to pass that you are offered the choice of things, see to it that you choose the simplest."

More than that the wise man would not say, so Aura went home and straightway prepared his canoe, persuaded Anaitu to go with him, and presently they set off.

The way was fearful enough, as the maiden had said, for much of it was through dark forests and between high river banks where the tree roots reached out black and twisted like evil serpents. Again, they had to pass through swamps where alligators slept and strange yellow beasts with heads large as houses lay hidden. And for many long hours they wound in and out of tangled jungles where the sun never shone and in the depths of which were strange things that roared so that the very trees trembled.

After many days they came to a smooth stretch of sand, and then the maiden told him that they had arrived in the land of her father.

"And now I must leave you," she said, "but my mother will come and offer you one of three things. See to it, dear Aura, that you choose wisely, for all depends upon your choice." At that she waved him a farewell and went up the bank and so passed from his sight.

Before long there came down the bank a wrinkled old woman with sorrowful eyes, and she bore three gourds. Setting them down by the side of the canoe, she bade Aura choose one. On the top of one gourd was a cover of gold, on the second a cover of silver, and on the third a cover of clay. Lifting the covers, Aura saw in the first fresh blood. In the gourd with the silver top he saw flesh, and in the third, a piece of cassava bread. Aura bore in mind the words of the old hermit and quickly chose the gourd that held the bread.

"You have done well," said the old woman. "This is a land where men believe in gold alone, and much blood is spilled because of it. Far better is it that men should choose that which is in the earth. Now having so chosen, I will lead you to my husband, whose name is Kaikoutji. But here cruelty reigns everywhere and he may tear you to pieces."

Aura had no mind to do otherwise than go through with his task and so told the old woman. Whereupon she led him to the top of the bank, where he again saw his Anaitu, and the maiden and her mother hid Aura in a forest near the house, while they went in to prepare Kaikoutji for the visit. Hearing that the young man who loved his daughter was near, the old man fell into a most marvellous rage and so great was his anger that he rushed out and bent trees as though they were reeds and bit rocks as a man bites a crust of bread. So there was much trouble before he was persuaded to see the gentle Aura. Even then, Anaitu begged Aura to return, but he threw his arms around her and was gone before she could say a word.

Strange things happened as he ran to the house. Great branches broke and fell without hands touching them and stones leaped from the earth and whizzed close to his ears, but he hastened on and entered into a hall. Kaikoutji was not there; but as Aura looked round, he came in running. The bewitched old man was strangely decked out with bones and teeth which dangled at the ends of strings fastened to his arms and legs and his head was covered with a great calabash painted green, in the front of which were two holes pierced, through which he looked. For a moment Kaikoutji stood, then giving a terrible howl he began to leap about, waving his arms and rattling the dangling bones and teeth—a very painful sight to Aura. The howling the man made was terrible. After much of this he stopped, turning the holes of his calabash on Aura.

"What can you do?" he yelled. "What can you do? Can you bend trees? Can you bite rocks? Can you leap like this?" Again he commenced to dance up and down, each leap being higher than the one before it, so that at last his calabash struck the roof.

When he had quieted down again, Aura said:

"I cannot leap. I cannot bend trees and I cannot bite rocks as you do. But I can work with my hands and make whatever you wish made."

Hearing that, Kaikoutji whirled about and gave three mighty leaps, rattling his bones and dangling teeth furiously.

"Make me a magic stool," he shouted. "And carve it of wood, with the head of a jaguar at one end and my head carved at the other. And see to it that you have it finished by sunrise, or else you die." Then he gave a yell, whirled about and rushed from the hall.

Aura saw that the task would be hard, even if he did what he had been set to do in the quiet of his own home. But without having seen the face of Kaikoutji he wondered greatly how he would complete his work. For all that he took his knife, selected a block of wood and went to work, and he worked with such a will that by midnight he had it all finished but the rough place at the end where was to appear the likeness of Kaikoutji. So he went to the old wife who had brought him the gourds and begged her to describe the features of her husband. But that she refused to do, saying that if she did so, Kaikoutji, who knew everything, being an enchanted man, would kill them all. An hour passed and everything was the same, Aura's work unfinished, his will as strong as ever. Then to him came the gentle maiden who took him by the hand and led him into another chamber where the old man sat in a corner asleep, his green calabash over his head. In another corner of the room was a hammock and into that Aura crept, thinking that if he kept quiet and remained hidden, by some chance the calabash might fall off and the face of the man be seen. But after looking long and seeing no move on the part of the sleeping man, he grew weak and weary.

Out of the corner near him came a small voice which said:

"From forest and hill
We come at your will.
Call, Aura, call!"

and looking that way he saw a mouse. At that the heart of Aura was glad, the more as he saw the mouse run to the sleeping man and begin to nibble at his hand. For a moment it looked as if Kaikoutji would take off his calabash, for he was plainly annoyed. But instead, by chance, he set his hand on the mouse, caught it, and flung it to the end of the room.

Again a voice was heard and this time Aura saw a spider dropping from the ceiling, and as it dropped it said:

> "From forest and hill
> We come at your will.
> Call, Aura, call!"

Over to the sleeper ran the spider, but matters were no better than before, for Kaikoutji dropped his hand, caught the spider, and threw it after the mouse.

No sooner had Kaikoutji fallen asleep again than there came into the room ants by hundreds and thousands, and leading them was the queen ant who sang:

> "From forest and hill
> We come at your will.
> Call, Aura, call!"

Like little soldiers they marched on the sleeper, swarming over his hands, his body, his legs. Under the calabash they went, a half hundred of them. That was too much even for Kaikoutji, and he leaped to his feet, dashed the calabash to the earth, and fell to brushing off the ants in lively manner. But the calabash was broken to pieces by the force of the fall, and for the rest of that night he slept with his face exposed.

From his hiding place it did not take long for Aura to learn his ugly features. Nor did it escape his notice that between the eyes was an arrow mark, and by that he knew that Kaikoutji was also the alligator he had shot in the lake. When he was sure that the old man was asleep, he slipped out quietly and went to his work, and with such spirit he wrought that before sunrise he had carved the face on the end of the stool.

Better still, so exact was his work, that all who saw it knew the face of Kaikoutji the terrible. But when the old man saw it and noted the arrow mark between the eyes, he leaped higher than he had ever leaped before, having no calabash to hinder him, and declared that the task had been too easy and that another must be done.

"Build me," he said, "a house of feathers before sundown, and see to it that there is no bird in the forest from which there is not a feather taken." Then, giving strict orders that no one should enter the part of the forest in which Aura was put, he leaped up and down several times, screaming horribly, after which he hastened away.

When all was quiet, Aura lifted his head and sang:

> "From forest and hill
> Oh, come. 'Tis my will.
> I call. I call."

Then there was a great rushing sound and from everywhere came birds: sea birds and land birds, river birds and lake birds, birds that flew, ran, and waded. There were sober brown birds, and birds more glorious than the rainbow. There was a cloud of humming-birds, glittering like powdered gold, and there were proud ostriches. Chakars dropped from the sky singing, and blood-red flamingoes raced with golden-crested wrens. There were songbirds, and silent birds, and birds whose cry was like the sound of a golden bell. There were storks, hawks, vultures, condors, swans, lapwings, and mocking-birds.

Not a moment did they lose. In and out and round about they went, weaving wonderfully, their busy beaks at work, and before an hour had passed there stood the most wonderful house of feathers that the eye of man ever saw. In the light of the sun it shone green-gold, violet, purple, brown, white, and scarlet. And when the last feather was woven the condor called, and the beating of so many wings, as the birds left, made the very air throb. When all was again silent it seemed to Aura that the work had been done in the twinkling of an eye.

The minute the sun touched the edge of the world Kaikoutji came howling and leaping. When he saw the feather house he stood for a moment with open mouth. So angry he was at the sight that his tongue was dry and parched and he could say nothing. But the glory of what he saw dazzled and blinded him, and with a howl he turned and plunged into the depths of the forest and was seen no more. Some say that he was drowned in the Lake of Pitch.

But Aura and Anaitu lived in the house of feathers and from that day to this the people of that land have been kind and gentle and have forgotten the evil days when cruelty reigned everywhere. Also, they know now that there are things more glorious than gold.

NA-HA THE FIGHTER

IN THE Far South near Cape Horn there is a place of
many islands, and it is a corner of the world where winds
are piercing cold and great black clouds scurry across a lead-
gray sky. From snowclad mountains slide rivers of ice from
which break off mighty pieces to fall into the sea with
thunder-sounds. It is a land wrinkled into narrow valleys that
are always gloomy and cold and wet. Cold, ice cold, is the
gray-green sea, and the wild cries of a million sea-birds fill
the air. Sometimes great albatrosses sweep up the channels
between the high, jagged mountains or drop low to sail over
penguin-crowded rocks, and sometimes the mountain echoes
are deep-toned with the booming of walrus and the barking
of seals. But people are few. There are Indians there, poor
gentle folk who fish in the sea and who know nothing but a
life of cold, and they paddle or sit crouching in their canoes,
taking no heed of the biting wind and the snow that falls on
their naked bodies.

Travelling in that part of the world, I came upon a boy

who had been left, somehow, on an island not much larger than a good-sized playground. He must have been there alone for some months, for he had lived on mussels and shell-fish, and the empty shells formed a good-sized heap about his sleeping place. Though I questioned him closely later, when we came to know one another, I could never learn how he got there. He was, I suppose, about ten years old, and certainly bright and intelligent. As for his memory it was quite remark-able, and he picked up words and the names of things very rapidly. Altogether, he stayed with me for three months, and I was often astonished at the aptness with which he did some things, as, for instance, the making of an arrow head from a piece of broken bottle. But other things he seemed quite un-able to do. A knot in a rope puzzled him sorely and for a long time a belt-buckle was a deep mystery to him.

One day I found that he was trying to tell me a story about a seal, for we had seen several that morning. For awhile I paid no attention, being occupied at something or other that required care, but soon it dawned on me that he was very earnest and that the tale was a long one. Fearing that I had missed much by my preoccupation and carelessness, I made him tell it to me a second and a third and a fourth time, and presently made shift to piece things together and so get a fair notion of his story.

I have called the tale by the name of the hero and have set it down in my own words and as I understood it. Were I to write it in his words it would go something like this:

"Many day, a far day, underwater man walk water. Eat man my father's father; men cry much hard." There would have to be indicated, too, much gesticulation and arm waving by way of illustration and emphasis. . . . So here is the tale.

Long years ago, the people of that land were sadly at the mercy of the wild, hairy folk who lived under the sea. To be sure, there were long periods when they were left in peace to do their fishing, though from their canoes they could look down into the waters and see the under-sea people walking on the sands at the bottom, very shadowy and vague, though, in the greenish light. Still, it was clear enough, for those who watched, to see their hair-covered bodies, their long and serpent-like arms and their noseless faces.

But again, there were times when the under-sea men marched in great numbers out of the water and caught the land men, dragging them down to their deaths. In such numbers they came that there was no resisting them. Nor was there escape, for the under-sea people could walk on the water, going faster than the wind itself. With earsplitting booming they would form themselves into a wide circle about the canoes, then draw nearer in wild rushes or strange slidings and drag the frightened men into the green-gray water. Sometimes a few only were taken and those that were left, looking down, might see the under-sea folk dragging their fellows to great rocks to which they bound them with ropes of leathery kelp.

One day the under-sea people caught Na-Ha, a youth strong as a wild wind, whose muscles were knotted like oak branches, one who smiled when danger came. Five of the noseless people attacked him and of the five, Na-Ha sent three to the bottom of the sea with broken necks, for though he smote them with his clenched fist alone, they staggered back and swiftly sank, and the blood that gushed from their mouths made a spreading pink cloud in the water. But soon the sea was alive with wild, raging faces and the roaring of them was like the southeast wind in the forest trees, yet

Na-Ha stood in his little canoe, cold and calm, and the smile did not leave his lips. Stealthily they crept toward him, none at first daring to attack, until with a fierce noise and clamour all rushed together, leaping upon him in his canoe and bearing it down by sheer press and weight, Na-Ha in the midst of the tangled mass of hair-covered creatures. Some who saw that fight said that the sudden silence when the waters closed over them hurt the ears like a thunder clap, but the true hearted Na-Ha was the last to disappear, and while he smote the black-haired ones furiously, the smile of scorn was still on his face.

Like a picture in a dream some saw the fight among the rocks at the bottom of the sea, saw the noseless ones crowding about the lad, saw others leaping over the heads of those who did not dare to near him, saw others again creeping in the sea sand, trailing kelp ropes to bind him. Many fell in that battle under the sea and the low waves that lapped the shore were red with blood that day. How it ended none knew, for with the dying light and the sand clouds that hung in the water all became gray at last and then swiftly faded.

That night the land people wept for Na-Ha the untamed, Na-Ha whose spear was like lightning, Na-Ha whose canoe rode the waves like the brown storm-birds. Tales were whispered of how he never bent beneath a load, of how in the blackest night he drove his boat before the storm, of how once he swept out to sea after a great whale and slew it, so that his people were saved from the hunger-death.

But with the screaming of the morning sea-gulls Na-Ha came to them again, walking up out of the sea, and his face was set and stern. Nor did he say a word until he had eaten and thought awhile.

The tale he told was of the under-seas and of his wandering after the battle in which he left so many dead in bloody sand. He had been sore-pressed, he said, but had broken away and come to a door in a cave, which he entered. It was a vast cavern in which he found himself, so vast that he could not at first see the end, and the roof of it he never saw, it being lost in a strange, cool-green light. The floor of the place was of gold dust and silver sand, and out of it grew networks of white rocks about which swam fish of many gay colours, while everywhere seaweeds swayed in gently moving water.

Soon he came to a place where, on a seat of white, sat a woman with bent head, and she was fair of skin and her golden hair floated in the water like a cloud. Being bidden, Na-Ha told her the tale of the fight and how the earth people were woe-ridden because of the evil work of the under-sea folk.

Patiently she listened, her cheek on her hand and her eyes large with grief, and when Na-Ha had done she told him that there was but one way to free his people and that was the way of the white death. Much more she told him and then gave him a great sea-shell and made him know that when he blew it the great cold that lies under the seven stars would be freed and the under-sea people driven for all time to their own place. Then she stepped from her seat, and taking Na-Ha by the hand gazed at him long.

"Many there are, Na-Ha, who live not to know of the good that they do. He who looses the white death must himself be stilled. This I tell you, Na-Ha, lest your heart fail you," she said.

That was all, for he did not tell the tale of how he came again to the land, but he showed them the great shell and said that his mind was made up to free his own people, though he himself slept the sleep. At that the people set

up a great shout and there were not wanting those who
offered to sound the blast, saying that it were better for
Na-Ha to lead the people. But that Na-Ha refused, and added
that the under-sea woman had told him that before the blast
was blown all the land people should take themselves and
their belongings to a far land under the sun, for staying where
they were, it would do but small good to drive the under-sea
people to their own place for ever, seeing that they themselves must also be ice-stiffened.

Then arose a confusion of talk, many being unwilling to
leave the land where their fathers and the fathers of their
fathers had lived, but Na-Ha prevailed and overruled them,
and soon the day came when there was a great movement
and canoes were loaded and the land people set off for the
country under the sun. So Na-Ha was left alone.

Over the length and the breadth of the land Na-Ha walked,
to see if by mischance some had been left, but there were
none. And when the sea-hen and the albatross and the gull
and the brown storm-birds saw the hair-covered, noseless people come out of the sea, when with the black loneliness of
night the snow came and the land waters were prisoned under
glassy ice, when the morning sun looked on a world of rime
and crystal frost, then Na-Ha put the great shell to his lips
and blew a blast that woke the echoes.

So the world soon grew faint and sleepy and all living
creatures except the noseless ones fled or flew after the land
people, and there was strange stillness everywhere. Trees that
had been green grew horned and black and then ghost-white.
And the black wind came raging and furious, and grinding,
groaning ice-mountains swam in the sea and locked the land,
and hills were cased in beryl walls.

Seeing all that, for a time the under-sea folk were full of

delight, believing themselves to be masters of the land, but soon they feared the glistening white of the world, the black scurrying clouds, and the fast-thickening ice. So they sought the sea, but no sea was there, only thick-ribbed ice across which swept snow-laden, stinging winds, and instead of the quiet of the under-water there was the calm of the white death. Under the eaves of the rocks they crouched, but it was small help, for with the biting cold they shrivelled and shrank. Close they hugged themselves, their elbows thrust into their hairy sides, their legs bent, making themselves small. And thus they stayed, nevermore to be as they were. For in that great cold the under-water people became seals, and seals they remained.

Well and bravely stood Na-Ha while all this came to pass, scornful of the death that clawed at him. Nor did he lay down to die until the great cold had passed away and his people returned to find the under-water folk forevermore bound to their own place, powerless to harm, looking always with wide, wondering eyes, lest the mighty Na-Ha again steal upon them and bring the great white death.

THE MAGIC BALL

(A Tale of the Chuput Country)

A COLD-EYED witch lived in the Cordilleras and when the first snow commenced to fall she was always full of glee, standing on a rock, screaming like a wind-gale and rubbing her hands. For it pleased her to see the winter moon, the green country blotted out, the valleys white, the trees snow-laden, and the waters ice-bound and black. Winter was her hunting time and her eating time, and in the summer she slept. So she was full of a kind of savage joy when there were leaden clouds and drifting gales, and she waited and watched, waited and watched, ever ready to spring upon frost-stiffened creatures that went wandering down to the warmer lowlands.

This witch was a wrinkled creature, hard of eye, thin-lipped, with hands that looked like roots of trees, and so tough was her skin that knife could not cut nor arrow pierce it. In the country that swept down to the sea she was greatly feared, and hated, too. The hate came because by some strange magic she was able to draw children to her one by one, and how she did it no man knew. But the truth is that she had a magic ball, a ball bright and shining and of many colours, and this she left in places where children played, but never where man or woman could see it.

One day, near the lake called Oretta, a brother and sister were at play and saw the magic ball at the foot of a little hill. Pleased with its brightness and beauty Natalia ran to it, intending to pick it up and take it home, but, to her surprise, as she drew near to it the ball rolled away; then, a little way off, came to rest again. Again she ran to it and almost had her hand on it when it escaped, exactly as a piece of thistle-down does, just as she was about to grasp it. So she followed it, always seeming to be on the point of catching it but never doing so, and as she ran her brother Luis followed, careful lest she should come to harm. The strange part of it was that every time the ball stopped it rested close to some berry bush or by the edge of a crystal-clear spring, so that she, like all who were thus led away, always found at the moment of resting something to eat or to drink or to refresh herself. Nor, strangely enough, did she tire, but because of the magic went skipping and running and jumping just as long as she followed the ball. Nor did any one under the spell of that magic note the passing of time, for days were like hours and a night like the shadow of a swiftly flying cloud.

At last, chasing the ball, Natalia and Luis came to a place in the valley where the Rio Chico runs between great hills, and it was dark and gloomy and swept by heavy gray clouds. The land was strewn with mighty broken rocks and here and there were patches of snow, and soon great snow flakes appeared in the air. Then boy and girl were terror-struck, for they knew with all the wandering and twisting and turning they had lost their way. But the ball still rolled on,

though slower now, and the children followed. But the air grew keener and colder and the sun weaker, so that they were very glad indeed when they came to a black rock where, at last, the ball stopped.

Natalia picked it up, and for a moment gazed at its beauty, but for a moment only. For no sooner had she gazed at it and opened her lips to speak than it vanished as a soap bubble does, at which her grief was great. Luis tried to cheer her and finding that her hands were icy cold led her to the north side of the rock where it was warmer, and there he found a niche like a lap between two great arms, and in the moss-grown cranny Natalia coiled herself up and was asleep in a minute. As for Luis, knowing that as soon as his sister had rested they must set out about finding a way home, he sat down intending to watch. But not very long did he keep his eyes open, for he was weary and sad at heart. He tried hard to keep awake, even holding his eyelids open with his fingers, and he stared hard at a sunlit hilltop across the valley, but even that seemed to make him sleepy. Then, too, there were slowly nodding pine trees and the whispering of leaves, coming in a faint murmur from the mountainside. So, soon, Luis slept.

Natalia, being out of the blustering wind, was very comfortable in the little niche between the great stone arms, and she dreamed that she was at home. Her mother, she thought, was combing her hair and singing as she did so. So she forgot her hunger and weariness, and in her dreamland knew nothing of the bare black rocks and snow-patched hills. Instead, she seemed to be at home where the warm firelight danced on the walls and lighted her father's brown face to a lively red as he mended his horse gear. She saw her brother, too, with his jet-black hair and cherry-red lips. But her mother, she thought, grew rough and careless and pulled her hair, so that she gave a little cry of pain and awoke. Then in a flash she knew where she was and was chilled to the bone with the piercing wind that swept down from the mountain top. Worse still, in front of her stood the old witch of the hills, pointing, pointing, pointing with knotty forefinger, and there were nails on her hands and feet that looked like claws.

Natalia tried to rise, but could not, and her heart was like stone when she found what had happened. It was this: while she slept, the witch had stroked and combed her hair, and meanwhile wrought magic, so that the girl's hair was grown into the rock so very close that she could not as much as turn her head. All that she could do was to stretch forth her arms, and when she saw Luis a little way off she called to him most piteously. But good Luis made no move. Instead, he stood with arms wide apart like one who feels a wall in the dark, moving his hands this way and that. Then Natalia wept, not understanding and little knowing that the witch had bound Luis with a spell, so that there seemed to be an invisible wall around the rock through which he could not pass, try as he would. But he heard the witch singing in her high and cracked voice, and this is what she sang:

> "Valley all pebble-sown,
> Valley where wild winds moan!
> Come, mortals, come.
>
> "Valley so cool and white,
> Valley of winter night,
> Come, children, come.
>
> "Straight like a shaft to mark,
> Come they to cold and dark,
> Children of men!"

Then she ceased and stood with her root-like finger upraised, and from near by came the voice of a great white owl, which took up the song, saying:

> "Things of the dark and things without name,
> Save us from light and the torch's red flame."

Now all this was by starlight, but the moment the owl had ceased, from over the hill came a glint of light as the pale moon rose, and with a sound like a thunderclap the witch melted into the great rock and the owl flapped away heavily.

"Brother," whispered the girl, "you heard what the owl said?"

"Yes, sister, I heard," he answered.

"Brother, come to me. I am afraid," said Natalia, and commenced to cry a little.

"Sister," he said, "I try but I cannot. There is something through which I cannot pass. I can see but I cannot press through."

"Can you not climb over, dear Luis?" asked Natalia.

"No, Natalia. I have reached high as I can, but the wall that I cannot see goes up and up."

"Is there no way to get in on the other side of the rock, dear, dear Luis? I am very cold and afraid, being here alone."

"Sister, I have walked around. I have felt high and low. But it is always the same. I cannot get through, I cannot climb over, I cannot crawl under. But I shall stay here with you, so fear not."

At that Natalia put her hands to her face and wept a little, but very quietly, and it pained Luis to see the tears roll down her cheeks and turn to little ice pearls as they fell. After a while Natalia spoke again, but through sobs.

"Brother mine, you heard what the owl said?"

"Yes, sister."

"Does it mean nothing to you?" she asked.

"Nothing," he replied.

"But listen," said Natalia. "These were the words: 'Save us from light and the torch's red flame.'"

"I heard that, Natalia. What does it mean?"

"It means, brother, that the things in this horrible valley fear fire. So go, brother. Leave me a while but find fire, coming back with it swiftly. There will be sickening loneliness, so haste, haste."

Hearing that, Luis was sad, for he was in no mood to leave his sister in that plight. Still she urged him, saying: "Speed, brother, speed."

Even then he hesitated, until with a great swoop there passed over the rock a condor wheeling low, and it said as it passed: "Fire will conquer frosted death."

"You hear, brother," said Natalia. "So speed and find fire and return before night."

Then Luis stayed no longer, but waved his sister a farewell and set off down the valley, following the condor that hovered in the air, now darting away and now returning. So Luis knew that the great bird led him, and he ran, presently finding the river and following it until he reached the great vega where the waters met.

At the meeting of the waters he came to a house, a poor thing made of earth and stones snuggled in a warm fold of the hills. No one was about there, but as the condor flew high and, circling in the air, became a small speck, Luis knew that it would be well to stay a while and see what might befall. Pushing open the door he saw by the ashes in the fireplace that someone lived there, for there were red embers well covered to keep the fire alive. So seeing that the owner of the house would return soon he made himself free of the place, which was the way of that country, and brought fresh water from the spring. Then he gathered wood and piled it neatly by the fireside. Next he blew upon the embers and added twigs and sticks until a bright fire glowed, after which he took the broom of twigs and swept the earth floor clean.

How the man of the house came into the room Luis never knew, but there he was, sitting by the fire on a stool. He looked at things but said nothing to Luis, only nodding his head. Then he brought bread and yerba and offered some to Luis. After they had eaten the old man spoke, and this is what he said:

"Wicked is the white witch, and there is but one way to defeat her. What, lad, is the manner of her defeat? Tell me that."

Then Luis, remembering what the condor had said, repeated the words: "'Fire will conquer frosted death.'"

"True," said the man slowly, nodding his head. "And your sister is there. Now here comes our friend the condor, who sees far and knows much."

"Now with cold grows faint her breath,
Fire will conquer frosted death."

Having said that the great bird wheeled up sharply.

But no sooner was it out of sight than a turkey came running and stood a moment, gobbling. To it the old man gave a lighted brand, repeating the words the condor had spoken.

Off sped the turkey with the blazing stick, running through marsh and swamp in a straight line, and Luis and the old man watched. Soon the bird came to a shallow lagoon, yet made no halt. Straight through the water it sped, and so swiftly that the spray dashed up on either side. High the turkey held the stick, but not high enough, for the splashing water quenched the fire, and seeing that, the bird returned, dropping the blackened stick at the old man's feet.

"Give me another, for the maiden is quivering cold," said the turkey. "This time I will run around the lake."

"No. No," answered the man. "You must know that when the water spirit kisses the fire king, the fire king dies. So, that you may remember, from now and for ever you will carry on your feathers the marks of rippling water."

Down again swooped the condor and a little behind him came a goose, flying heavily. As before, the condor cried:

> "Now with cold grows faint her breath,
> Fire will conquer frosted death,"

then flew away again toward the witch mountain.

To the goose the old man gave a blazing stick and at once the brave bird set off, flying straight in the direction the condor had taken. Over vega and over lagoon she went, pausing only at a snowclad hilltop, because the stick had burned close to her beak. So she dropped it in the snow to get a better hold, and when she picked it up again there was but a charred thing. Sad enough the goose returned to the house, bearing the blackened stick, and begged to be given another chance.

"No. No," said the old man. "The silver snow queen's kiss is death to the fire king. That is something you must remember. From now on and for ever you must carry feathers of gray like the ashes. But here comes the condor and we must hear his message."

Sadly then the goose went away, her feathers ash gray, and the condor wheeled low again, calling:

"Fainter grows the maiden's breath,
Night must bring the frosted death,"

and having said, like an arrow he shot off.

No sooner had he gone than the long-legged, long-billed flamingo dropped to the ground.

"Your beak is long," said the old man, "but fly swiftly, for the stick is short."

The flamingo took the burning stick by the end and made straight for the mountain, racing with all possible speed. As for Luis, he made up his mind to tarry no longer and set off, running like a deer. But an ostrich, seeing him, spread her wings like sails and ran by his side. On her back Luis placed his hand, and with that help sped as fast as the flamingo. In the air the flamingo went like an arrow, resting not, although the blazing fire burned her neck and breast until it became pink and red. But that she heeded not. Straight up the valley and to the rock where Natalia was bound went she, and into a heap of dried moss on the south side of the rock she dropped the blazing stick. Up leaped the dancing flames, and with a tremendous noise the rock flew into a thousand pieces and the power of the witch was gone for ever. As for Natalia, she was at once freed, and with her gentle, cool hand stroked the breast of the flamingo so that the burns were healed, but as a sign of its bravery the bird has carried a crimson breast from that day to this.

As for Natalia and Luis, they lived for many, many years in the valley, and about them birds of many kinds played and lived and reared their young, and the magic ball of the witch lived only in the memory of men.

THE HUMMING-BIRD AND THE FLOWER

GOOD morning, pretty flower!"
G "Good morning, little humming-bird!"
"May I have some honey, please?"
"Certainly. Here is plenty. Help yourself."
"Thank you. It is very good of you. Is there anything that I can do for you in return?"

"Well, I hear so little, seeing that I do not go abroad, that I love to be told things. I wish that you would tell me how you came to have so beautiful a dress. I have often wondered as I saw you flashing past."

"Have you indeed? Well, let me think. I believe I have heard that it was because of a mouse, that I have it."

"A mouse? How can that be, busy little Colibrí? A mouse, you know, is dull and gray."

"Then, Florecilla, if it was not a mouse, it was mud."

"My dear humming-bird, you *must* be wrong. You know as well as I do that mud is dull and gray. Won't you stop your humming a moment and think?"

"Ah, now I know. It was because of a panther."

"Dear, dear Colibrí, that is worse still. A panther, did you say? I must have heard wrong."

"Isn't that right, either? Well, it must have been all three —the mouse, the mud, and the panther. So there now. . . . But how sweet this honey is."

"Indeed, I am glad that you find it so. But please tell me about your pretty dress."

"Oh, yes. I forgot, thinking of the honey. One has so much to think of. I remember now, perfectly well. It was Paloma the dove who told me all about it yesterday, but a day and a night is a very, very long time to remember a long tale."

"Then tell me before you forget."

"Well, once all humming-birds were gray."

"So I have heard."

"Well, a big panther was going through the woods very quietly, and he stepped on a mouse-nest and happened to kill all the baby mice."

"Dear me. I am so sorry to hear that."

"So when the mother mouse came to her home and saw what had happened she was very much annoyed, saying that the panther was too big and too clumsy and did not look where he was going."

"Well, Colibrí, she would be annoyed. You know I have often thought how nice it would be if mice and panthers and all creatures did not move about as they do. They run about so and they jump and skip, and it is no wonder that things happen. Suppose trees and flowers and bushes were as restless as animals. Think how it would be with great trees treading on little flowers, and thorn bushes running about and tearing down the gentle flores del aire and scratching the tender skins of the grapes. Now if *I* were queen, I would make a law so that all those forest creatures that run on four legs should just stand and grow as we do, and——"

"Please do not interrupt or I may forget the tale."

"Oh, I beg your pardon. Go on, please."

"Well, of course the panther told the mother mouse how it had happened and said that he was sorry and that he would be more careful, but she scolded him and kept it in her heart to punish him."

"But, little Colibrí, if he said that he was sorry, and if it could not be helped, then it seems to me——"

"Really, little flower, you *must* listen. You have no idea how difficult it is to tell a tale. So please do not interrupt. One day when the panther was asleep the mouse crept up with some gum which she had taken from the tree and sealed up the panther's eyes. Then she took mud from the laguna and plastered it over the gum, and then more gum and more mud, so that the panther could not tell day from night."

"Dear me. That was very unkind and very dreadful. I am as sorry for the panther as I am for the mother mouse."

"Well, anyway, that proves that it was a mouse and a panther and mud, just as I said."

"But, dear humming-bird, how about the dress of many colours?"

"I am coming to that, but you interrupt so. The panther roared and roared and roared, until the very softest of his roars shook the esteros, and the alligators were frightened and dived to the bottom of the water. Hearing all that noise, a humming-bird asked the panther what the noise was all about."

"That was very good of the humming-bird. And what did the panther say?"

"He told the humming-bird all about it and asked him to

kill the mouse. But that the humming-bird would not do."

"Of course not. *I* never killed a mouse."

"So then the panther said that if the humming-bird would take away the gum and the mud so that he could see again, he would do anything that he could in return. You see, little flower, the panther is wise because he travels so much and all things that travel know a great deal."

"I am not so sure of that, Colibrí. All this summer I have travelled up this tree and so have gone a great distance, but I know very little."

"That is different. No one wants a flower to be wise. To be beautiful is enough."

"Oh!"

"But please listen and do not talk so much."

"I am very sorry that I interrupted you, little humming-bird."

"Well, the humming-bird told the panther that she wished to have a beautiful dress, as beautiful as the dress of the sun bird, and asked him to tell her where she could get bright colours. Then before the panther answered, she asked him to tell her how the lianas got the red and yellow and purple for their blossoms."

"This is the most interesting thing I have ever heard and I hope the tale will not be short. Did the panther know?"

"Of course he knew. He told her that the flowers got their colour from the earth and he also told her where there was clay of many colours and where there were gold and silver and rubies. So the humming-bird picked and picked until the panther's eyes were unsealed and the big fellow gave a roar of gladness. All that day panther and humming-bird worked, bringing coloured clay and coloured sands, and silver and gold, and rubies and opals, and the blue and crimson of sunset and the silver of the moon and the stars, and the tender green of shady forests and the blackness of ebony. Out of all these the humming-bird dressed herself, and for misty-moving wings she took the spun silk of the spider and the soft thread of the sumaha. And that is how the humming-bird got her dress. There now."

"I am glad to know that, dear humming-bird, and I thank you for telling me."

"And I, dear flower, thank you for the honey."

"Good-bye, then, if you must go."

"Good-bye, Florecilla. . . . *B-z-z-z-z. H-m-m-m-m-m—mm-mmmm.*"

EL ENANO

EVERYONE disliked El Enano who lived in the forest, because he always lay hidden in dark places, and when woodmen passed he jumped out on them and beat them and took their dinners from them. He was a squat creature, yellow of skin and snag-toothed and his legs were crooked, his arms were crooked, and his face was crooked. There were times when he went about on all fours and then he looked like a great spider, for he had scraggy whiskers that hung to the ground and looked like legs. At other times he had the mood to make himself very small like a little child, and then he was most horrible to see, for his skin was wrinkled and his whiskers hung about him like a ragged garment.

Yet all of that the people might have forgiven and he might have been put up with, were it not for some worse tricks. What was most disliked was his trick of walking softly about a house in the night-time while the people were inside, suspecting nothing, perhaps singing and talking. Seeing them thus, El Enano would hide in the shadows until someone went for water to the spring, then out he would leap, cling-

ing fast to the hair of the boy or man and beating, biting,
scratching the while. Being released, the tortured one would
of course run to reach the house, but El Enano would hop
on one leg behind, terribly fast, and catch his victim again
just as a hand was almost laid on the door latch. Nor could
an alarm be raised, because El Enano cast a spell of silence,
so that, try as one would, neither word nor shout would
come.

Then there was his other evil trick of hiding close to the
ground and reaching out a long and elastic arm to catch boy
or girl by the ankle. But that was not worse than his habit
of making a noise like hail or rain, hearing which the people in the house would get up to close a window, and there,
looking at them from the dark but quite close to their faces,
would be the grinning Enano holding in his hands his whiskers that looked like a frightening curtain, his eyes red and
shining like rubies. That was very unpleasant indeed, especially when a person was alone in the house. Nor was it much
better when he left the window, for he would hop and skip
about the house yard for hours, screaming and howling and
throwing sticks and stones. So, wherever he was there was
chill horror.

One day, a good old woman who lived alone went with
her basket to gather berries. El Enano saw her and at once
made himself into a little creature no larger than a baby and
stretched himself on a bed of bright moss between two trees
leafless and ugly. He pretended to be asleep, though he
whimpered a little as a child does when it has a bad dream.

The good old woman was short-sighted but her ears were
quick, and hearing the soft whimper she found the creature
and took it in her arms. To do that bent her sadly, for
Enano when small was the same weight as when his full size.

"Oh, poor thing," she said. "Someone has lost a baby. Or perhaps some wild creature has carried the tender thing from its home. So, lest it perish I will take care of it, though to be sure, a heavier baby I never held."

The dame had no children of her own and, though poor, was both willing and glad to share what she had with any needy creature. Gently she took it home and having put dry sticks on the fire she made a bed of light twigs which she covered with a mat of feathers. Then she bustled about, getting bread and milk for supper for the little one, feeling happy at heart because she had rescued the unhappy creature from the dismal forest.

At first she was glad to see the appetite of the homeless thing, for it soon finished the bread and milk and cried for more.

"Bless me! It must be half starved," she said. "It may have my supper." So she took the food she had set out for herself and El Enano swallowed it as quickly as he had swallowed the first bowl. Yet still he cried for more. Off then to the neighbours she went, borrowing milk from this one, bread from that, rice from another, until half the children of the village had to go on short commons that night. The creature devoured all that was brought and still yelled for more and the noise it made was ear-splitting. But as it ate and felt the warmth, it grew and grew.

"Santa Maria!" said the dame. "What wonderful thing is this? Already it is no longer a baby, but a grown child. Almost it might be called ugly, but that, I suppose, is because it was motherless and lost. It is all very sad." Then, because she had thought it ugly she did the more for it, being sorry for her thoughts, though she could not help nor hinder them. As for the creature itself, having eaten all in

the house, it gave a grunt or two, turned heavily on its side
and went to sleep, snoring terribly.

Next morning matters were worse, for El Enano was
stretched out on the floor before the fire, his full size, and
seeing the dame he called for food, making so great a noise
that the very windows shook and his cries were heard all
over the village. So to still him, and there being nothing to
eat in the house, the good old woman went out and told
her tale to the neighbours, asking their help and advice, and
to her house they all went flocking to look at the strange
creature. One man, a stout-hearted fellow, told El Enano that
it was high time for him to be going, hearing which, the
ugly thing shrieked with wicked laughter.

"Well, bring me food," it said, looking at the man with
red eyes. "Bring me food, I say, and when I have eaten
enough I may leave you. But bring me no child's food, but
rather food for six and twenty men. Bring an armadillo
roasted and a pig and a large goose and many eggs and the
milk of twenty cows. Nor be slow about it, for I must
amuse myself while I wait and it may well be that you will
not care for the manner of my amusement."

Indeed, there was small likelihood of any one there doing
that, for his amusement was in breaking things about the
house, the tables and benches, the pots and the ollas, and
when he had made sad havoc of the woman's house he
started on the house next door, smashing doors and windows,
tearing up flowers by the roots, chasing the milk goats and the
chickens, and setting dogs to fight. Nor did he cease in his
mischief until the meal was set out for him, when he leaped
upon it and crammed it down his throat with fearful haste,
leaving neither bone nor crumb.

The people of the village stood watching, whispering one

to another behind their hands, how they were shocked at all that sight, and when at last the meal was finished, the stout-hearted man who had spoken before stepped forward. "Now sir!" said he to El Enano, "seeing that you have eaten enough and more than enough, you will keep your word, going about your business and leaving this poor woman and us in peace. Will you?"

"No. *No.* NO!" roared El Enano, each No being louder than the one before it.

"But you promised," said the man.

What the creature said when answering that made nearly everyone there faint with horror. It said:

"What I promised was that I would leave when I had eaten enough. I did not——"

The bold man interrupted then, saying, "Well, you have eaten enough."

"Ah yes, for one meal," answered the cruel Enano. "But I meant that I would leave when I have eaten enough for always. There is to-morrow and to-morrow night. There is the day after that and the next day and the next day. There are to be weeks of eating and months of eating and years of eating. You are stupid people if you think that I shall ever have eaten enough. So I shall not leave. No. *No.* NO!"

Having said that, the creature laughed in great glee and began to throw such things as he could reach against the walls, and so, many good things were shattered.

Now for three days that kind of thing went on, at the end of which time the men of the place were at their wits' ends to know what to do, for almost everything eatable in the village had gone down the creature's throat. Sad at heart, seeing what had come to pass, the good old woman went out and sat down to weep by the side of a quiet pool, for it seemed

to her to be a hard thing that what she had done in kindness
had ended thus, and that the house she had built and loved
and kept clean and sweet should be so sadly wrecked and
ruined. Her thoughts were broken by the sound of a voice,
and turning she saw a silver-gray fox sitting on a rock and
looking at her.

"It is well enough to have a good cry," he said, "but it is
better to be gay and have a good laugh."

"Ah! Good evening, Señor Zorro," answered the dame, dry-
ing her tears. "But who can be gay when a horrible creature
is eating everything? Who can be otherwise than sad, seeing
the trouble brought on friends?" The last she added, being
one of those who are always saddened by the cheerlessness
of others.

"You need not tell me," said the fox. "I know everything
that has passed," and he put his head a little sideways like a
wise young dog and seemed to smile.

"But what is there to do?" asked the dame. "I am in serious case indeed. This alocado says that he will make no stir
until he has had enough to eat for all his life, and certainly
he makes no stir to go away."

"The trouble is that you give him enough and not too
much," said the fox.

"Too much, you say? We have given him too much already, seeing that we have given him all that we have," said
the old dame a little angrily.

"Well, what you must do is to give him something that he
does not like. Then he will go away," said the fox.

"Easier said than done," answered the old woman with
spirit. "Did we but give him something of which he liked
not the taste, then he would eat ten times more to take the

bad taste away. Señor Zorro, with all your cleverness, you are but a poor adviser."

After that the fox thought a long while before saying anything, then coming close to the old woman and looking up into her face he said:

"Make your mind easy. He shall have enough to eat this very night and all that you have to do is to see that your neighbours do as I say, nor be full of doubt should I do anything that seems to be contrary."

So the good old woman promised to warn her neighbours, knowing well the wisdom of the fox, and together they went to her house, where they found El Enano stretched out on the floor, looking like a great pig, and every minute he gave a great roar. The neighbours were both angry and afraid, for the creature had been very destructive that day. Indeed, he had taken delight in stripping the thatched roofs and had desisted only when the men of the place had promised to double the amount of his meal.

Not five minutes had the fox and the dame been in the house when the men of the place came in with things—with berries and armadillos, eggs and partridges, turkeys and bread and much fish from the lake. At once they set about cooking, while the women commenced to brew a great bowl of knot-grass tea. Soon the food was cooked and El Enano fell to as greedily as ever.

The fox looked at Enano for a while, then said:

"You have a fine appetite, my friend. What will there be for the men and the women and the children and for me to eat?"

"You may have what I leave, and eat it when I end," said El Enano.

"Let us hope then that our appetites will be light," said the fox.

A little later the fox began to act horribly, jumping about the room and whining, and calling the people lazy and inhospitable.

"Think you," he said, "that this is the way to treat a visitor? A pretty thing indeed to serve one and let the other go hungry. Do I get nothing at all to eat? Quick. Bring me potatoes and roast them, or it will be bad for all of you. The mischief I do shall be ten times worse than any done already."

Knowing that some plan was afoot the people ran out of the house and soon came back with potatoes, and the fox showed them how he wanted them roasted on the hearth. So they were placed in the ashes and covered with hot coals and when they were well done the fox told everyone to take a potato, saying that El Enano, who was crunching the bones of the animals he had eaten, would not like them. But all the while the men were eating, the fox ran from one to another whispering things, but quite loud enough for Enano to hear. "Hush!" said he. "Say nothing. El Enano must not know how good they are and when he asks for some, tell him that they are all gone."

"Yes. Yes," said the people, keeping in with the plan. "Do not let Enano know."

By this time El Enano was suspicious and looked from one man to another. "Give me all the potatoes," he said.

"They are all eaten except mine," said the fox, "but you may taste that." So saying he thrust the roasted potato into the hands of Enano and the creature crammed it down its throat at once.

"Ha! It is good," he roared. "Give me more. More. MORE."

"We have no more," said the fox very loud, then, quite softly to those who stood near him, he added, "Say nothing about the potatoes on the hearth," but loudly enough for El Enano to hear, though quite well he knew that there were none.

"Ah! I heard you," roared El Enano. "There are potatoes on the hearth. Give them to me."

"We must let him have them," said the fox, raking the red-hot coals to the front.

"Out of the way," cried El Enano, reaching over the fox and scooping up a double handful of hot coals, believing them to be potatoes. Red hot as they were he swallowed them and in another moment was rolling on the floor, howling with pain as the fire blazed in his stomach. Up he leaped again and dashed out of the house to fling himself by the side of the little river. The water was cool to his face and he drank deep, but the water in his stomach turned to steam, so that he swelled and swelled, and presently there was a loud explosion that shook the very hills, and El Enano burst into a thousand pieces.

THE HERO TWINS

THERE was once a woman who had two sons and they were twins, so much alike that the mother herself could not tell one from the other. So Hunapu always wore a crimson feather and Balanque a blue one.

As children they spent their days in the open air, playing in the forest, swimming in the lake, and wandering on the plains, and so doing they came to know the animals and the birds, finding the young ones and playing with them, so that it was no uncommon sight to see them come home with a panther following at their heels as a dog does. They knew where to find the nests of birds of all kinds, fed the young ones, and petted them, until with a call they could bring from the trees clouds of glorious-coloured birds which would perch on their hands and arms and shoulders. And of course it came about in time that when animals and birds gathered about the lads, there was no more fighting between the wild creatures than there is between a puppy and a kitten that have been raised together.

Growing up with the wild creatures, wrestling with them

and racing with them, the boys grew strong and fleet of foot. They could scale a cliff to reach a condor's nest or climb a tree as swiftly as a monkey, and in the water they were as much at home as on the land. Down into the clear depths they would dive, down in the cool, green lake waters, to bring up shells and bright stones, one boy striving with the other, laughing merrily the while. And sitting on the shore in the sunshine they would often look across the lake to the far-away mountain, talking about the time when they would adventure there to see what could be seen.

Their father taught them to shoot straight with the arrow and to use well the spear, and when they were masters of these he made for them breastplates of silver and light helmets that flashed in the sun. And as time went on they wandered here and there, finding other boys of their own age, and these, too, had helmets and breastplates of silver made for them by their fathers and had learned the use of the bow and spear, until at last there was a band of four hundred of which Hunapu and Balanque were leaders. Then there were great times with running and racing and swimming and wrestling, and soon the Four Hundred had agreed that when one of their number was in trouble not of his own seeking, at the sound of the horn the rest would come to his rescue. But not all the time was spent in play, for the band of the Four Hundred were wise in all the arts, playing the flute, working in metals, painting, woodcraft, and other like activities.

One day Hunapu and Balanque were in the forest gathering fruit, when there came to them an old man and wife, weeping sadly. They were strangers to the place and, seeing the two lads in their armour of silver, with bows in their hands and swords by their sides and feathers of crimson and of blue in their glittering helmets, they stood for a while silent. But being asked, they told their tale of how they had lived in the mountain on the other side of the lake among a people who were in terror of their lives because of three great and fearful giants who came now and then, taking the cattle and the goats, destroying for mere mischief the houses of the people, and sometimes killing the people themselves. Nothing, they said, could withstand the strength of the giants. Stone walls were as mere sticks to them. They uprooted trees or turned the courses of rivers by scooping away masses of earth with their hands.

Hearing that, the twin brothers were greatly disturbed, for as they had sat by the lake sometimes, talking of the land far away, they had heard strange noises faintly come over the waters, which they had set down as summer thunders. With the tale of the old man and his wife, they began to believe that things were more serious than they had supposed. Stepping to a place clear of trees Hunapu put his horn to his lips and blew long and loudly, three times. Soon from all directions came lads running, each girt with his sword, his spear in hand and his bow at his back, breastplate and helmet glittering in the bright sun. You can figure for yourself that fine band of clean, straight-limbed fellows, each with his drawn sword and silver helmet with drooping plume. You can imagine how they looked standing there with the cool, green forest behind them. And there were not only the Four Hundred, but also their friends of the forest, here a puma, there a panther or deer, bright-coloured birds, glorious humming-birds and proud llamas, for not a boy but had his wild creature for a pet.

To the band of the Four Hundred the old man and his wife told their tale, mentioning what they had not done be-

fore, that their sons and daughters had been carried off by
two of the giants. At that there stepped from the ranks a lad
with flashing eyes who said that not a year should pass over
their heads before the giants were overcome, and a great
shout of joy went up. Then and there the lad who had spoke
cried:

"Let everyone step forward who will go to the land of the
evil three," and no sooner were the words out of his lips than
the whole Four Hundred stepped forward. But, as Flashing
Eyes said, some must stay at home, for there were things to
be done, so he proposed that twenty alone should go. Even
then there was no way to decide which of them should be of
the twenty, for everyone wanted to go forward to the adventure. At that Balanque offered to go alone to the land, to see
what would be the best plan to pursue, but again there was
trouble, for each of the Four Hundred wanted to go with
him. So at last it was decided to leave the matter to be set-
tled by chance. Each one was to call to his pet wild creature,
and the first two touched would go to the land of the giants.
Then a great calling went up, a naming of names, a whistling, and a making of noises like the call of animals, and
from the leafy caves came the pets, running, leaping, flying.
Each lad there had hung his sword and bow on a branch
and stood with arms outstretched to welcome his pet, and
there was much laughter and good spirit. Down from the sky
came sweeping a hawk, straight as an arrow, and it lit on the
shoulder of Balanque. At the very same moment a llama
thrust its nose into the neck of Hunapu, and that only a second before a fleet deer had leaped to the side of Flashing
Eyes. So all there knew that the twin brothers were chosen
to go into the land and there was no more arguing about it.
That night the band slept under the brilliant stars and the

next morning there went up a great shout as at sunrise the brothers set off, every one of the Four Hundred knocking his sword on his shield by way of salute. From the top of a ridge the twins waved their band a farewell, then they turned and a moment later were lost to view, and the members of the band went each about his own affairs, ready to come at a call.

All that day and the next they travelled, and on the morning of the third day they came to a place where were great black rocks, and hills all treeless and bare, and near the noon hour they saw a great cave in the mountainside, the floor of which was strewn with bones of animals, some of the bones indeed being great things as big as a man, from a creature of which the boys had never seen the like. These bones had been cracked for the marrow in them and the teeth marks told their tale of the size of the giant who had eaten them.

To a top of the mountain the boys climbed, and when they had gained the summit, there at their feet was a great hollow place and at the other end sat a monstrous fellow, his hands on his knees, his body swaying to and fro. He was rumbling and grumbling and peering here and there in a queer way. The boys noticed that he did not turn his head to look with a sweep of the eyes as they did, or as you do, turning to see in a semi-circle or over a greater extent. His way was different. He would turn his head in a certain direction with his eyes closed, then open them and look. From the place where his glance lit he could not turn. If he wanted to look somewhere else, he had to close his eyes and begin again, so that his looking was more like shooting a bullet at a mark than anything, and if he missed, he missed, and had to begin again. And of course he often missed. Yet it was his way, and he must have been very satisfied with it to judge by the song he sang, which was this:

"My name is Cakix,
Yukub—Cakix.
My eyes are bright as silver,
They gleam like precious stones.
My name is Cakix,
Yukub—Cakix.
Cakix!
Cakix!"

Over and over again he sang that. Then, with a tremendous roar, he shouted:

"I am Cakix,
Yukub—Cakix,
And all men fear me!"

Then the twins, hearing that idle boast, stood on the hilltop and shouted:

"Catch us, Cakix, if you can. We come to make an end of you."

For a moment the giant sat still in sheer astonishment, his eyes closed, his ear cupped in his hand to catch the direction of the sound. The boys saw his great face turn in their direction, and they skipped to the right and left so as to be out of his sight, and well it was that they did so, for out over the valley shot his arm, lengthening like elastic, and his great fingers reached over the rock where the twins had stood, and went feeling like five blind snakes. Finding nothing, the hand picked up the rock, though it was as large as a house, and back went the arm getting shorter, until the giant had the rock under his nose. Then he shut his eyes, turned his face down, opened his eyes again, and examined the rock. Finding nothing he cast it away with a sudden jerk, much as you jerk off some insect that drops on your hand unexpectedly.

Cakix sat awhile, then rose to his feet and strode straight down the valley to where the boys had been, looking straight ahead, of course. He went to a tree a little way off, plucked some fruit which looked like wild cherries, though each was as large as a pumpkin, and blundered off without seeing the boys who crouched low and out of his sight.

As soon as the giant had gone the twins ran down into the valley and there they saw, in great caves in the hills to the right and left, hidden heaps of flashing, precious stones —diamonds, emeralds, rubies, opals—dazzling in the sunshine. In other holes were heaped gold dust and silver. While looking they were startled to hear a new roaring, this time from the hill to which Cakix had gone. Soon the roar formed into words and they heard:

> "I am Cabrakan,
> Cabrakan who shakes the earth,
> Cabrakan who shakes the sky.
> I am Cabrakan,
> Master of men."

It was another giant, but him they did not see. Scrambling out of the valley they reached the hilltop to see Cakix coming back to his valley. He stopped at the tree where he had stopped before and took some more fruit, then strode down the hill, marking time as he walked with his:

> "I am Ca-kix
> Yu-kub—Ca-kix
> All men fear me."

He sat down in his old seat, his hands again on his knees, his body swaying. He seemed uncomfortable and restless, much as if he expected danger, getting to his feet every now and then, peering about, going to his tree to eat fruit and returning again to his seat. In fact, about every hour he went to his fruit tree.

Seeing that, the lads had an idea, and running to the fruit tree, climbed into it, hiding themselves in the thick branches, but no sooner were they safely there than they heard the monster coming.

In a very short while they felt the tree shake with the giant's heavy tread, for he was on his way to take another meal. Then in less time than it takes to count six he was at the tree, his great blue face hiding the scenery. Quick as lightning, Hunapu fitted an arrow to his bow, drew the string to his bow, and let fly. The shaft struck the ugly fellow in the chin, but so tough was his skin that the barb only pierced to his jaw. Still, the pain of it was enough to send him away roaring. Back he went to his valley and threw himself down, groaning and weeping. There was no loud song from him now.

The boys descended from their tree and marched down to where Cakix lay, taking good care to keep out of the way of his great kicking feet.

"Who are you?" asked the giant when he saw them. "And what do you want here?"

"We are doctors," they answered. "Hearing your roar of pain, we came to help. It is your teeth that need attention. Let us take out your bad teeth and you will be at ease."

"But my teeth are my strength," said the giant. "Men do not know it," he added with the lack of suspicion of all giants.

"True," answered the twins. "We will pull out the old teeth and put new ones in their place."

The giant opened his mouth and to work they went with hammers and bars of iron, and in a short time had his teeth all out. True to their promise they put new teeth in place of the old, but the new teeth they fitted were made of grains of corn, and as soon as Cakix tried to eat with them he found out his error. So in a short while he died from starvation, and the earth was rid of one of the monsters.

There was great joy among the band of Four Hundred when the hero brothers returned and told their story, for they were glad of the good fortune of the twins and full of rejoicing that the world had one monster the less in it. And after a week of resting, there came a day when the whole band, bright in their polished armour and gay with feathers and flowers, set off for the Stone Mountain to bring back the treasures and to slay the remaining giants. But the tale is so long and so interesting, that it must be left for another chapter.

THE FOUR HUNDRED

SINGING and waving banners, the four hundred youths
with the twin brothers at their head, all of them slim
and well formed, brown of skin and straight of limb, marched
forth to the land of the giants, their eyes bent on the far
mountains all wrapped in a blue, floating mist. No faint hearts
were there, nor among them were bullies or cowards. Not one
there but could run, leap, shoot straight, and look his friend
in the eye. From shields of silver the sunlight flashed, spear-
heads were like points of hard light and each helmet was
plumed. Bows were slung across shoulders and swords were
at sides, and sandalled feet marched in step. No food they
bore nor were they otherwise burdened, for well each knew
the way of the forest and the trick of lake and stream; well
each knew the fruit-bearing trees and the bushes that were
berry-hung, and at night their roof was the star-sprinkled sky.

Straight as an arrow was their course to the west, to the
land of vast rocks, and gullies like axe-clefts in the earth.
Straight to the west, not turning for swift-flowing stream nor
yellow marsh; plunging through forest, climbing mountain,

scaling cliff. Straight to the west to the place where the twin brothers had been before, until they came to the valley of Cakix and saw his bones already white, picked by carrion birds. There, too, they saw the caves where were heaps of glittering diamonds, rubies like fire, emeralds cool green like the caves of the sea. Gold, too, and silver were there, but no heed gave they to all that, counting such things but as toys for children, when great things had to be done.

Scouting far and wide to hilltop and rocky ridge, going by twos in vast circles until they met again, they swept the land, seeing sign of neither Cabrakan nor of the giant Zipacna, and when the band met again all were prepared to fare farther in their quest. None was for returning, "for," said they, "there is an evil thing to put out of the land and the swifter the foul task is done the better."

The second day of their quest they came to a great forest and there they were set upon by great monkeys that came in hundreds and tens of hundreds, leaping at them and snarling, baring teeth and fiercely chattering. For a while it looked of ill omen, but knowing that together they could meet much the Four Hundred formed a square, so facing north and east and south and west, a line of lads kneeling with pointing spears, others behind them with spears over the shoulders of those that knelt. In vain the apes dashed at them, for not a spear was lowered nor did heart grow faint. But the air throbbed with the cries of the hairy things and they came in ever-increasing numbers, striving to break by sheer weight the spear-bristling square. All that day they came, hurling themselves against the square until the dead things lay in masses, those that were wounded screaming in pain and anger as they turned again to the forest, and when the dropping sun touched the hills and the green became black, the evil things, finding their work in vain, gave up the fight and fled snarl-ing.

So the Four Hundred all unharmed, weary, though light of heart because of the great fellowship that was shown to be among them, shouldered their spears, re-slung their bows and marched on, until coming to a noisy stream they washed themselves and their weapons. Then in the white moonlight they slept, each with his sword at hand, while some watched, on guard for that which might threaten.

When the sky was rose-tinted again they went on their way, making for a narrow pass like a sword-slash in the mountains, and by noon they had reached the stony cut. High and bare were the white rocks on either side and gloomy was the pass, nor of living thing was there sign save a condor wheeling high. But from the rocks came strange noises, whis-tlings and screamings, then of a sudden, like a thunder clap, a mighty roar as from many voices, and the noise of it echoed and re-echoed from rock to rock so that the din was deafen-ing, and when they spoke one to another, mouth went to ear and hands were cupped. Then, when they were well within the pass, marching over a floor so covered with sharp-pointed rocks and great round boulders that they had to slacken their pace, there came from above a great rock which fell ahead of their path so as to block the way, except for a narrow passage on either side. Looking up, they saw, crowded on the tops of the high cliffs on every hand, snag-toothed, evil-eyed fellows who crawled about the rocks as though they had been lizards, so sure of foot were they. They knew then that they were in the land of the wild men of the mountain, the crag men, fellows strong and stark, full of hate and viciousness.

Of a sudden, from one of the creatures who stood far up in the cleft of a rock, one whose hair and beard were long

and white and tangled, came a hoarse cry, and lifting high
above his head a rock greater than ten armadillos he cast it
downward with great force. Ill would it have been for any
youth struck by it, but so badly and swiftly was it thrown
that it passed over the heads of all, struck the wall on the
farther side, and burst into a hundred pieces. So the youth
with the bright eyes called on his fellows to hold their shields
above their heads, edge to edge and overlapping in such wise
as to form a roof, which they did. Well it was thus, for stones
rattled down like hail, some so great that those on whom they
fell were almost borne to earth with the sheer weight, for the
men of the crags were many and strong. Yet the weight being shared by reason of the jointed shields, all went well,
for each youth's care was for his fellow.

In one place the pass ran narrow, and there one of the
crag men, a fellow of great animal strength and swiftness,
suddenly leaped down and bore one of the twin brothers to
earth by the violence of his flight through the air, for the men
of the crags leaped from rock to rock like wildcats. It was
Balanque who was thus struck down, but he was on his feet
in an instant, drew his sword hastily, and as the crag man
rushed at him with jaws all foam-flecked and horrible he
passed his blade through the crag man's chest. But the fellow
was like a wild boar, pressing on regardless of the hurt, so
that he ran up onto the hilt, caught the youth by the waist,
and flung him over his shoulder. In a moment more he would
have been on his way up the face of the cliff. As it was, seeing what had come to pass, the crag men set up a great yell-
ing and screaming, thinking that victory already lay with their
man. But Bright Eyes was not idle. He fitted an arrow to
his bow and let fly, the shaft passing through the crag man's
neck, so that he stood, as it were, spitted, and let Balanque

fall. Pierced though he was with both arrow and sword, yet there was life in him and he fled to the rock face and clambered up, leaving a trail of red wherever he passed, and was seen no more by any of the band.

No pause all this while was there in the shower of stones, but, shields well locked, the band pressed on, foot by foot, each youth stern to win and proud of his companion, each youth keeping the eye of hope on the thin, bright strip of blue at the end of the pass where the mountains would fall away. And there they came at last, toil-worn but heart-strong, to the plain where the crag men dared not follow, some of them almost weeping for joy because shoulder to shoulder they had again fought their way through a great danger and an evil place, where, had but one failed, all might have been lost.

There were four hundred and two happy youths that night, though the place where they slept was bare of grass and trees, and in the morning they were well rested and strong, for as they had lived well and cleanly and none having a darkened window in his breast, their sinews were as steel, and every day was a new life in which to enter with eyes bright and shining.

The sun had not far risen; indeed, there seemed but a hand's breadth between the lower edge of it and the world's edge, when a great wonder appeared before their eyes. It was as if the sun were suddenly blotted out, for what they had taken to be a low, faintly rising hill in the east had risen up, stood for a moment like a vast cloud, then passed swiftly to the south. At the same time there came a roar like thunder from the cloudlike form, which came near to deafening them. And the roar formed into words:

"I am Zipacna whom men cannot slay,
There's naught that I fear save the watery way."

That rolled rumblingly as thunderings between earth and
sky, now loud, now softer, as Zipacna strode from valley to
valley. A little later he came in sight again, but far to the
north of where they were, then vanished from their sight
into the cleft of the hills where they had battled with the
crag men.

Now fearful as was the sight of the giant, yet no fear was
in any heart, so, having made a meal and rested for a season,
without more to-do they set off for the place from which the
giant had arisen. It was long before they got there, but at
last they stood on the edge of a long and narrow cañon at
the end of which was a mighty pile of bones, not alone of
animals but also of men, and there were human skulls there
and shells of sea-crabs, and in and among all these crawled
venomous serpents. But most of all were there sea-crab shells.

While they gazed at this sorrowful sight, there came to
them a bent old woman, sad of face and lined and wrinkled,
and her talk was more like croaking than human speech.
Secret and watchful was she in her manner. To the twin
brothers and Bright Eyes, who stood a little apart from the
rest of the band, she spoke, asking them:

"What do ye here, my fine fellows? And why come ye
to this place of evil and misery?"

One of the three answered boldly that they came to slay
the giant Zipacna, telling her that he was a thing of evil
and that evil things must be laid low if the world is to be
fair.

"Then," said she, "ye are doubtless prepared to die, for
in times past many have thought to slay Zipacna, but them-

selves have been led into feasting and into pleasure and soft living, and so the memory of the good that was intended, passed and became less than a dream."

Her words they found strange, but she went on to tell them of a land over the hill where all was fair and where none had to work and where the sun shone. There seemed but little meaning in her words.

But they made answer, saying: "We have but one desire, which is to slay Zipacna for the evil that he has done and must do. As for your land of fine things, if to live there would make us soft and idle, then must our eyes be closed to it."

Hearing that, the old woman seemed pleased and the shadow of a smile touched her face. But her manner changed swiftly it seemed, for she shot a question at them which was this: "You passed the caves of Cakix whose bones now are white? Give me then of the precious stones that lay in the caves there," and so saying, stretched forth her skinny arm, her hand hollowed to receive gifts.

"It was not for such toys that we came. We saw but touched not the precious stones, nor the gold, nor anything that was there. Indeed, to have done so would but have hampered us in the doing of that which we set out to do." Thus Hunapu made reply and the others nodded.

"And how did ye escape the apes of the forest?" she asked.

"We stood side by side and met danger."

"And the men of the crags, how fared ye with them?"

Bright Eyes answered quietly: "Each covered himself and his neighbour as well as he could and so we came out with whole skins."

A silence fell then, the three saying nothing because of the woman's great age, though her words and questions seemed to lack meaning. What she said further was a greater riddle still. "It was well done," she told them, and nodded slowly. "Now a greater task lies before. It is one in which each of your band must meet danger separately and to his peril, if eyes are not lit and feet swift. More than that I cannot tell. But go onward until the sea is reached and there is a lake of water. Whoso touches that water is turned to stone, so take heed. But well indeed will it be if Zipacna is led there. Have ye not heard him sing:

> I am Zipacna whom men cannot slay.
> There's naught that I fear save the watery way?

Heard ye not that at sunrise?"

Then she said no more but turned away. Now as she took a step her staff fell from her unsteady hands and Bright Eyes picked it up and gave it to her. That seemed to open her lips again, for she told them:

"Hearken, one and all. Many are there like swine, who live but to eat, and Zipacna is of that sort. Watch well by the sea shore to the end that ye see the things that may lead to his destruction." There was no more. She passed down the hill and disappeared behind a thorn-bush and at the moment that she vanished from their sight a white puma leaped out from the other side, by which they saw that she knew of white witcheries.

The band lost no time in turning their steps seaward, and although the day was hot and the place inviting, would not rest in a valley through which they passed, a place rich in fruits and soft with silk grass. That evening they came to the sea, and at the foot of a cliff saw a great lake of water so clear and blue that their eyes could follow, dropping from rock ledge to rock ledge, down the slope of the side until they saw the stones and the sand on the bottom. But there were no swaying water-weeds, nor was there living thing. Another thing they saw which brought the words of the old woman to their minds, for thrown aside on the beach were hundreds and thousands of sea-crab shells, from which they knew that it was the sea-crab that Zipacna loved to eat above all things.

Now they also saw that by some chance a great tree had fallen, and one end of it rested in the water of the lake, and that end had turned to stone. Another thing they saw, for on the farther side of the lake was a bed of blue-black clay and the colour of it was the colour of the shell of a sea-crab. So after some thought and some talk many of the lads went deftly to work fashioning of the clay a great sea-crab, so great that the like was never seen. Others dragged to the lake straight tree-trunks which they laid side by side with the tree already there, and the end of the stick was turned to stone as soon as it touched the water, the rest of the tree changing more slowly. All that night they wrought, making the great crab and setting it on the sloping tree-trunks, so that when morning broke, that which they had set out to do was finished, and while it was yet gray dawn they set off for the place where Zipacna dwelt.

But not all the band went. Here a lad was left, a little way off another, then another and another, each hiding behind rock or tussock or thornbush or tree. So hid, one by one, fifty, a hundred, two hundred, until at last there were left Balanque, Hunapu, and Bright Eyes. Then at the foot of a hill Bright Eyes sat down and Hunapu crouched on the shoulder of another hill that stood alone. So, the band being all hidden, it fell out that Balanque alone went to the place where they had met the old woman. He fell to making a great outcry, calling on Zipacna to come forth and rattling his sword on his shield merrily.

"Oh! Coward!" he called. "Come forth and be slain as was your brother Cakix, whose bones are now scattered and white."

In a voice of thunder Zipacna cried:

"I am Zipacna whom men cannot slay.
There's naught that I fear but the watery way."

Over and over he chanted that, now roaring, now grumbling as grunts a swine when it would rest. But always Balanque taunted him, calling him a coward giant, telling him that his days were short, and reminding him of the fate of Cakix.

At last the slow blood of the giant was on fire and he rose on his elbow to look. For a time he saw nothing, being slow of sight and moreover looking too high, little dreaming that his noisy champion was so small. When he saw Balanque at last, his hand shot out, but Balanque was swift, and like the wind fled at top speed to where his brother Hunapu lay. Down dropped Balanque and up sprang Hunapu, clearing the ground like a deer, with Zipacna in full chase, the giant little dreaming that he was following a new man. But Hunapu, fresh and rested, did as his brother had done and sped to the foot of the hill where Bright Eyes lay. Then like an arrow went Bright Eyes to the thornbush where Huno was, and Huno in his turn darted to the tree where Chimal rested. So also Chimal raced, and each of the band did the same when his turn came, the giant Zipacna following, no more knowing one lad from the other than one ant can be told from its fellow. And in the rear those who had dropped to hide gathered again, so that three companions became five,

five became ten, and ten became fifty, while over hill and valley and marsh, through thorn-thicket and wooded hill, Zipacna rushed, each lad leading him on his dance, each companion rising from his resting place, ready and swift. And so each of that band met danger alone to the end that all might be safe.

At last the merry chase led Zipacna to the cliff, and there below him he saw what he took to be a mighty crab on the tree-trunks, ready to drop into the water of the lake, and at the sight of it his mouth watered and his eyes grew large. A touch of his foot sent the crab sliding into the water, and to save it Zipacna thrust out his hand. But he bent never to straighten again. Solid and firm was he fixed, the crab a crab of stone, his hand a hand of stone. Solid and firm was he fixed, a crouching giant in a crystal lake, where he stands to this day.

As for the band of Four Hundred, many other valiant deeds did they in the land, but through all, never was the thread of their fellowship broken or tangled, and if evil threatened one, then no rest of stay had the others until all was well again.

RAIRU AND THE STAR MAIDEN

PERHAPS my friend Pedro of Brazil told me the story of Rairu and the Star Maiden for much the same reason that hungry men fall to talk of meals that they have eaten. When I say hungry men I do not mean men with an appetite, but men who have long been on the verge of starvation—shipwrecked sailors, men lost in the desert, and such like. The truth is that what the heart hungers for, the tongue talks of. So my friend Pedro told me many tales of his own warm land where spice-laden breezes blow gently soft, and at the time he told me his tales we two were in the midst of the snows of Tierra del Fuego, when the winds shrieked like a thousand demons and the frost-giant had bound river and lake.

We were gold digging on the upper Santa Maria and there came without warning a fierce blizzard, the snow falling for the best part of two days and two nights, and in the morning we could not move from our tent, though we had pitched it in a quiet nook of the hills. We had little to eat, nothing to read, and no light but the fire-glow, and the world seemed to narrow about us, the mountains to close in and the leaden sky to drop. And all the while Pedro talked of his gentler land, telling me the glory of hills all purple and green, of sunlit waters and flower-crowned children. So, soon we forgot the black south wind and the destroying cold. Pedro half forgot, I think, that hope which led him to the Far South; it was a hope long cherished, that he might find gold enough to enable him to live in quiet in his own land among the books that he loved.

However, you may think this wearisome talk, judging it better that I tell the tale told by Pedro. But I have felt it best to set it down as I have, because Pedro never saw his own land again; so the writing of the story is in some measure done in affection for my friend. As soon as the snow ceased to fall he went away on foot, our horses having wandered before the storm, and his intention was to win his way to a shack some eight miles away where he might get some food which we needed sorely enough. I in the meantime, we agreed, would take my rifle and try to shoot a huanaco or some other thing. But another storm came on and it was not until five days had passed in search that I found Pedro. And he was frozen.

As I write I see the scene again—the snow-swept hills, the gray sky, the white-laden bushes, and Pedro. I made what haste I could to bury him in the icebound earth and put up a rough cross to mark the place, and I had barely finished when a white storm swept up and hid both mound and cross.

Here is the tale he told, one of many, and he said that he had heard it often and often when he was a child.

The Tale

Of all things, nothing pleased Rairu more than to watch the ways of the living things of the forest, to bend over a

flower and drink in its beauty, to lie by the side of a leaf-hidden pool and follow some shaft of sunshine as it shot to the depth, or to stand breathless when a wild bird broke into song. His father, very bitter against what he deemed idleness, often said harsh things, telling Rairu that he would do well to attend to matters more enduring. Still, Rairu was what he was. Before the sunlight came over the world he would seek the forest deeps and there, hidden in green thickets, would lose himself in the music of the birds. And as time passed and Rairu grew into young manhood another joy came to him, and the glory of the star-sprinkled sky filled him with wonder. Night after night he would wait in a favourite place by a little cascade, a place bare of trees, eagerly impatient for the soft light of the first star in the violet sky.

Watching thus Rairu found a thought rise in his mind, a thought that the world would be well only when that order was among men which was in the skies. More, it seemed to him that of all living creatures that walked the earth man was the most destructive, the most wasteful, and the most untrustful. Then one night as he lay at the foot of a palm tree, his heart was full of gladness because of the song of a night-bird, and it came to him somehow to believe that the stars sang to the bird as the bird sang to the stars, so he looked up to find, if possible, which star heard that bird, and he saw one that hung low, one far more beautiful than her fellows. Thereafter, when the sky grew soft and dark, his eyes sought the Silver One and he waited until the night-bird sang. Like jewels, like living sparks of sound, the music went up, and like a maiden the Silver One listened. When the star dropped in the west and the song-bird ceased, then Rairu was sad and alone, alone as one in a seagirt land whom none may visit.

One day, it was a day of cloud-flecked sky and humming

life, Rairu met an old man, thin-haired and bearded, and the stranger hailed him, calling him by name. After some talk, much of which seemed riddlesome to the lad, the old man asked him what of all things, had he his wish, would he choose.

After thinking awhile, Rairu said:

"If the Silver One would come from her place in the sky and go with me so that I might admire her beauty both day and night, I would be the happiest man on earth."

Hearing that, the old man bade Rairu go to sleep that night on a high hill which was not far away. "And," said he, "if it be that you desire the Silver One for her beauty alone and not that others may envy you in your possession, then it may be that your wish shall be granted." No more he said, but walked away, singing to himself softly as he went.

All that day Rairu spent in the forest, eager for the night and the stars, and in the noonday heat sat in the shade of the trees with eyes fast closed, trying to make a song in which he might tell the world of the Silver One and her great beauty, for it vexed him that so few looked to her; but no words came to him to satisfy. Only this, which he thought but a poor thing:

> When men sorrow and rage,
> When the hearts of men grieve,
> When arrows of sharp words wound,
> When there is none to pity pain,
> In the order of heaven there is sweet delight.

> In the night hushed and still,
> When is neither weeping nor laughter,
> In the night-time between two empty days,
> The Silver One is riding in the sky
> Singing hand in hand with her sister stars,
> Singing, because the life of men is an empty dream.

When darkness was about to spread he went up the rocky path to the hilltop, as the old man had bidden him, and lay there looking at the opal fires in the western sky, watching the change to sea-green and gold, from orange to pink, and waiting, waiting until the stars should come forth. Now and then he sang the lines of the song he had made, the last lines:

> In the night-time between two empty days,
> The Silver One riding in the sky
> Singing hand in hand with her sister stars,
> Singing, because the life of men is an empty dream.

When at last the stars pricked the dark, great was his grief to find that the Silver One was not among them. He searched well, thinking that she hid perhaps behind a leaf, but soon he knew that her sisters went their way alone. Long and long he looked, and at last, wearied and sad at heart, fell asleep, weeping that he had lost the thing to him most dear.

As he slept he dreamed that the earth was bathed in a great white light, a light that was both light and music, at which he became wonderfully happy. He dreamed that he was lifted up as on a cloud, lifted up high into the heavens and could see, far below him, countless sweetly turning spheres of light; and across great dark spaces and gulfs of blackness were other and new stars; and from the edge of nothingness to the edge of nothingness all was a-tune. Still, for all that, his heart was heavy, because in all the stardust there was no Silver One. What was most strange was this: though his heart was heavy, yet a joy was in him, a sad joy for that he felt himself as a tight-stretched golden string that quivered in tune with the music all about. So he awoke and saw standing by his side a maiden clothed in white, whose eyes looked into his heart with deep love.

"Arise, Rairu," said she, "for I have come to cheer and to comfort. I am the Silver One and you may keep me with you." So saying she became small, small but none the less beautiful, so small indeed that she might have stood in the palm of Rairu's hand.

Then Rairu was the happiest of mortals. He cast about him for a casket in which to keep his treasure, but finding none worthy, bethought him of his gourd, a thing which he had carved and adorned with much excellent skill. Having cleaned it well, so well that not a grain of dust was in it, he set it on the ground on its side in a clean place and the Silver One stepped into it, resting lightly on a bed of light green moss. All that day Rairu went about, now and then taking the cover from the gourd to look within and gaze with delight at the eyes of the Silver One looking up at him. Whenever he did that, from the gourd there came a sound of melting music, so entrancing a sound that Rairu felt himself to be a part of all things—a part of the very heavens and the stars and the sun and the moon. Even of the forest with its animals and birds, its trees and its pools, he was a part.

Day and night strange things the Silver One told Rairu, and of those things that which he found most sad was her telling that when the day came on which he took his eyes from her and thought of other things on which she would not look, things which hid from her in dark places and under roofs, then there would be a dividing and she would become to him but as an aching memory. At that Rairu, after pondering awhile, always laughed, telling her that no sword could sever the thread that bound them.

There came a day when the Silver One told Rairu that it would be well if they visited the sky-world for a season, and to do that Rairu was quite willing. So at her bidding Rairu sat among the leaves of a palm tree and the Silver One crept out of the gourd and took her place by his side. With a little stick she touched the tree, and at that it grew rapidly, grew until it carried them into a place all bare and treeless, without birds or flowers. The Silver One told Rairu to wait a while and she would return. She sped away and Rairu kept her in his sight, for her light did not dim.

Soon, to his astonishment he saw, close at hand, a beautiful city with shining towers and moving lights of many colours, and about it went a joyful procession of young men and maidens, dancing and singing and playing instruments. Many beckoned to him to follow them, which he did. Soon he came to a great hall, and as he entered a great burst of music sounded, whereupon all there fell to dancing, whirling wildly. Wilder and more wild grew the music; it became a welter of sound, a boiling flood of strange noise that set his brain on fire. From corners leaped evil and ugly things, bats, swine, evil-eyed carrion-birds, blunt-tailed and mud-coloured serpents and great white toads, soft and clammy. In the wild dance they joined and the din grew louder, so that it seemed to Rairu that his ears must crack. But more fearful things there were, so that Rairu fled to the place where he had stood when the Silver One left him.

She was there waiting for him, but her eyes, though still full of love, were filled with sad tears. Very gently she chided him for his disobedience, and Rairu hung his head in sorrow and shame, knowing that he must leave the Silver One for a season. It needed no words to tell that the thread was broken. Hand clasped hand then, the more passionately because they knew that there would be a parting.

"Go then, Rairu," said she. "But mind well that a little

toil, a little striving, and thou shalt find me again. In the darkness lean on me, the more because thou knowest thyself to be weak. Under the shadow of death, dear Rairu, a fainting love is revived."

So Rairu returned to earth, but great was his desire to find again that which he had lost. And he told his fellowmen of all that he had seen, saying that he must again find his star. Soon, with searching, he found his Silver One and the clear light led him, clothing all that he said and did with beauty.

THE TALE OF THE GENTLE FOLK

LET me see. This story begins at the time I climbed down the Andes on the east side and came upon a house by a lake. There were two children living there, one named Juan, the other, his sister, named Juanita, and the boy was seven years old and the girl nine. They had never seen a school, and the nearest house was more than fifty miles away. Still they had books, knew how to read, and I do not think that they ever found the day long. For one thing the lake was not at all deep, and a little bit off from the shore of it was a small island. That was a kind of playground for them, and often they paddled their boat to it in the early morning and stayed there all day.

There were other things highly interesting. On the second day that I was there, I saw their tame ostrich, a great gray bird that they had had for two years, and now and then Juan would ride it, Delicia, which was the name of the ostrich, spreading his wings like sails, and running out in a wide zigzag circle on the pampa, caring no more for the light weight on his back than a chicken would care for a fly. Some-

how, the birds of that place were no more afraid of the
children than the cat is afraid of you, and they knew places
where they could see the flamingo with its scarlet cloak, the
cowbird all glossy violet, the lapwings making a drumming
music, gray and white scissortail with feathers a foot long,
and red oven-birds. But their great pet was the huanaco, tall
and proud-looking, all yellow and white, like a camel without a hump, about the size of a donkey. They called him
Campeón, and he had been on the place as long as the children could remember. Their father, who owned many sheep,
had found him when he was no larger than a fox, brought
him to the house, and he had become as tame as a pet lamb.
Both Juan and Juanita would roll over on him as he lay in
the sun, burying their faces in his gold-coloured fur, hug-
ging his long neck, wrestling with him until he got up and
walked away to find a quieter place. They would use him as
a horse, harnessing him to a little wagon, and all would go
well sometimes, but sometimes not so well, for Campeón taking it into his head to run, the wagon would upset, the children roll out on the soft grass, and in a moment Campeón
would free himself from the harness, going in great leaps
to find a little hill where he would perch himself on the
crest and stand like a sentinel.

Now one day the man who was my travelling companion
was out with his rifle, and coming upon old Campeón standing on a high rock, took him for a strange and wild animal,
and, like many thoughtless men with a gun, followed his
impulse and shot. Campeón was badly wounded, and doubtless astonished to receive such treatment from the hands of
a man. Anyway he limped on three legs to the house. Juan
and Juanita grieved sadly, their parents no less, and all was
done for Campeón that could be done. As for my friend,

seeing what had happened, he was the most sorrowful of us all. For a time it seemed as though Campeón would get better, but one day he was plainly worse. All that day he rested on the sheltered side of the house, refusing food and water, his finely shaped head proudly upright, his eyes turned to the south, and the next morning there was no sign of him. From the hill on which he had stood we could see for miles and miles, and Juanita and I went there, taking a telescope, and we searched the country far and wide. In the afternoon we saddled horses and rode many, many miles until we came to a belt of sandy soil that ran east and west, and there we saw the trail of our Campeón going straight south. So we turned home sadly enough, for we knew that we would see the gentle beast no more.

And this is why: If you have read the "Arabian Nights," you will remember, in the story of Sindbad the Sailor, that it is told that he discovered a wonderful valley in which were the bones of hundreds and thousands of elephants. Whether there is any truth or not in that, I do not know, but I do know that in south Patagonia there is a vast valley called the Valley of the Gallegos and there the huanacos go to lay down their bones when they feel the coming of death. And beautiful Campeón, though he had never seen that valley, somehow felt that he must find it, being so wounded and sick, and while we slept that moonlight night, had left us. Both Juan and Juanita knew well enough that they would never see Campeón dead, for they had heard the story of the huanaco valley as often as you have the story of Cinderella. So had I heard it, and that night when we fell to talking about Campeón, a gaucho who looked after the horses told us the story again, and this is what he said:

Long, long ago, when there were giants and before there were horses in this land, there lived a gentle people who did not know sickness or pain or anger. They moved about among the animals and the birds as we move about among the flowers in the garden, and men were much kinder and the maidens more graceful and beautiful than any on the earth to-day. The colours of the birds were brighter and the scent of the flowers sweeter than now; the sun was never too hot nor the wind too cold. What was more wonderful, the Gentle People had a strange power by means of which they could change flowers into living things which turned to bright-coloured birds.

Now and then there would be great gatherings, when all the Gentle People would come together before their prince who sat on a throne decked with precious stones. And the people who loved him for his wisdom as well as for his goodness brought to him at such times gold and silver and diamonds and rubies and glittering precious stones, and these he would give to the young people to play with, for in those days people loved things for their beauty alone. The birds and animals too would join in the gathering, and the air would be full of song and colour and the scent of woods and flowers. On that day each person there would have his or her wish granted, whatever it was. To be sure, where was so much that was good, it seemed hard to wish for anything at all.

There was one thing only that was forbidden to the Gentle People, which was to go north until they saw no more the stars of the Southern Cross in the sky, for after many days' journey, they were told, there was a great dark forest on the other side of which were fierce men who did evil. But one day one of the Gentle People saw a strange bird, more beautiful than anything ever seen, a bird whose breast shone green and blue and gold, with a tail of long feathers white as ivory. Capa it was who saw the bird, and it seemed strange to him that seeing him the bird flew away. Never before had he seen a bird that he could not touch and hold, and the more the bird avoided him the more eager was he to take it to the prince. So he followed it as it went from place to place, always thinking that at last the strange bird would allow him to draw near. That it feared him he never knew, for his people knew no fear, neither did the animals nor birds that lived among them. At last the bird led him to the edge of the forest, and when he looked into the sky that night he saw new stars there, at which he wondered. Into the forest he went, always following the bird, and so tall and thick were the trees that the sun did not shine and the stars were blotted out at night.

Then one day he came to a place where he saw men with yellow skins and teeth like a dog, who gathered about him. Never before had he seen such people, who tore animals apart and ate of the flesh, who tore skins from living creatures and wore them on their own bodies. To make matters worse, these yellow-skinned ones seized Capa and took from him his glorious robes of gold and silver thread, tore the feathers from his hair and plucked away the ruby that he wore for its beauty. Then, greatly to his surprise, they fell on one another, fighting for the things that they had taken from Capa, so that the very robe they struggled for was torn and trampled under foot. At that Capa turned and fled back through the forest, never stopping day or night, until he came to his own people.

Straight to the prince he went and told his tale, hearing which, the prince was sad at heart.

"You have," he said, "been where there are greed and selfishness and avarice, and it is bad for us. For those of the yellow skin will not rest until they have found us and brought sorrow into our midst."

Then he called all his people together and they came, as they always did, singing and dancing and bearing flowers, and after them came the birds and animals, skipping and flying, calling. But a great silence fell upon all when they saw their Golden Prince, for his eyes were grave.

So he told the Gentle People all that Capa had seen, and Capa himself stood by the side of his prince and sang a sad song, so that the people knew of the evil on the other side of the dark forest, and the hearts of the Gentle People were as heavy as was the heart of the Golden Prince. And the prince told them that if they chose, he would arm them and lead them so that they could go forth and fight against the yellow-faced men when they came, "but," he went on to say, "having learned to fight and to do hurt and to bring death, then you yourselves will turn on each other, will bring death to your own people. You will turn against the animals and they will turn against you. You will walk the land alone, and all things will avoid and hide from you. These things of the earth, these bright and shining things which to-day you take or leave as you wish, you will play with no more, but will hide in boxes and under stones so that others may not see them." When he said this last he picked up a handful of diamonds and rubies, of emeralds and gold dust, and poured them from one hand to another, so that it was as a cascade that fell bright and dazzling in the sunlight.

Fearing that, the Gentle Folk looked at one another, and there was no doubt in their minds. "Far better," said they, "is it that we should change in some manner and flee away than that we should do evil to the birds and beasts that are our friends."

Then the Golden Prince called on his people to follow him, and as the yellow man broke through the forest as he had said they would, he led all of them away swiftly, and the multitude of animals and birds followed them. Having arrived at a great valley where was a river, he told his people that he would change their form so that they would become for a time other creatures, but creatures that would neither bite nor scratch nor spit poison, nor do any kind of harm. So he changed them into huanacos, animals of proud and graceful carriage, and their dress was of red and white like the gold and silver they wore. Then when he saw his people thus, friends of the birds and animals they loved, he changed himself into one also, but greater and more beautiful than any.

But there was a memory of that time, and even to this day when a herd of huanacos is seen, there also is one standing on a high rock as sentinel, keeping watch for the yellow men. And when at last the prince huanaco died, he died in the valley; seeing which, each of his people also laid down their bones in that place, as you may read in many books. So must it be until each and every huanaco has passed away. Yet remember this: Where dies a huanaco, there springs up a flower blue as the sky, its petals all gold-tipped. And when the day comes in which the last huanaco dies, then the yellow men will be gone. On that day each flower will bend to its neighbour and, at a word, there will stand a great host, for the spirit of the huanaco is in the flower that is blue and gold-tipped. Then, for ever and ever, the Gentle People will again have their land, and kindness and gentleness and beauty and joy will be theirs once more.

THE TALE THAT COST A DOLLAR

WE SAILED for many a day, Bob and I, up narrow channels and down wide ones, twisting and turning this way and that, east, west, north, south, because of wind and tide and cape and bay, and then we came to a kind of S-shaped strait. Through it we went and found that it opened into a wide water, as smooth as glass and so clear that we could see down to the sandy bottom where seaweeds clung to rocks and fishes swam in a strange greenish light. Then, by great good luck, we found a place where was deep water and followed the channel landward, and it turned out to be the cutting made by a stream of very cold water that came down from the mountain. So there was strange rowing for us, for we worked our boat into the rivulet which was so narrow that very often both oars were on the grassy land. When at last we stopped, it was because the banks came so close together that our boat blocked the passage, so we stepped to land as easily as one might step onto a wharf.

Next morning, having covered our things from the foxes and made all neat and shipshape, we set off on a walk, climbed a high ridge and looked for a while over a confusion of little islands and narrow straits, then wondered at the blue of sea and sky, and after that wandered down a long slope, to come soon to a pleasant valley, and the more we saw of it the better we liked it. It seemed to have everything desirable, soft grass, clear and cool water, shelter from the winds, and peaceful quiet. A half-dozen horses could be seen a little way off, and on a blue hill in the distance there were cows and sheep. Soon we heard the voices of children and the interlacing echoes. So we rounded the hill and came upon houses, four of them altogether and all thatched with yellow rushes. The children that we had heard we saw, and they were playing with a pet huanaco, and at one of the doors, seated on a rush-bottomed chair was an old woman whose face was wrinkled and brown, though her body seemed as supple as that of a young person. Seeing us the children left their play and stood, their dove-eyes full of wonder.

For the rest of that day we rested, enjoying the place. In the evening, when men and lads returned from their hunting or their fishing or their herding or whatever they did, there was good fellowship in the pleasant December twilight, and as we talked and sang we became better acquainted. Of course, like all travellers in that or any other open country, we had to tell the tale of our wanderings, how we came to be there and why, and when we had done, one or the other of them told us what might be said to be the history of their people, one helping the other out, correcting the talker when he was at fault, and sometimes taking the tale from him to tell it better.

They talked Spanish, for all were originally from Chile, and we learned that the old woman's husband, who was no longer living, had been a soldier who had fought against Peru and was on board a warship called the *Esmeralda* which was sunk by another, and on that sad day, she said, more than a hundred were drowned. A merciful Heaven permitted her husband to get ashore after much danger, and wandering, he had found the valley in which we then were (for having found it he had gone to his own place, which I took to be Ancud or somewhere near there), and with three neighbour families they had wandered, delighted to find a place where were no din and clashes and war. "And," said the old woman, lifting her hands and throwing them a little apart, "here by the grace of Heaven we are at peace."

When she had done the children chattered a little, insisting that she had missed the most interesting part of all. She should, they held, tell the strangers the tale of how the valley had been made, of why there was a river, of how it had come to pass that there were woods through which the river flowed and especially why Laguna Viedma was salt. The caballeros, they were sure, would like to know all that, it being a tale most wonderful and strange. But the old woman shook her head and made herself a cigarette, saying that it was a tale told her by a very, very old Indian woman who was there when she first saw the place, and the Indian had heard it from her mother, and she from her mother, and she again from her mother, so the tale went so far back that whether it had truth in it or not none could tell. At that the young people said that, true or not, it was a good tale, and they were so politely insistent, especially a little girl who petted a blue-eyed kitten, that we heard the story which, so far as I know, has never yet been written, and were it not written now might be forgotten for ever. So here it is, and my daughters, Julia and Helen, like it better than any story in this book, though their brothers are in favour of the tale of the Nose-less People.

Long ago, said the old woman, south of the Laguna Viedma lived a bruja, or kind of witch, a mean and wicked creature who had a house at the foot of the cordilleras built of great slabs of stone, in which there were three rooms. In one of these rooms she had imprisoned a boy and in another a girl, and the boy she allowed to roam about in the garden in the daytime but locked him up whenever the sun set, and the girl she locked up whenever the sun rose, so that the boy had never known night and the girl had never seen day, nor had the boy or the girl cast eyes on one another.

The boy, growing out of childhood, grew restless, and one day he dug a passage in his stone cell under the wall and up on the other side, much as a rabbit might have done, so that after being locked up he could spend a little time in the twilight, watching the dancing green stars that were fireflies. Still, whenever it grew dark and the edges of the things that he saw were no longer sharp, he scuttled back to his stone room, not knowing what clawed horror might unfold from the dark. For we must remember, said the old woman who told the tale, in all his life he had seen no human being but the witch, and knew no more of the moving world than the horses that we use know of the horses that drag a thousand noisy wheels in the city streets. Nor did he know of the ten thousand silver lights in the sky at night, nor of the bright glory of the Southern Cross.

One evening when the boy was in the vega, he having crawled through his passage, his heart fell when he saw a strange creature dressed in white, with long black hair and soft eyes. When the strange thing walked towards him he was startled, for he also saw the gray mist from which she came, and in that mist he seemed to see other thickening shapes. So, for a moment, he had a mind to kill the long-haired creature as an evil thing, and picked up a sharp stone, but his heart somehow bade him do otherwise, and he turned and fled, running straight to his hole by the side of the bush, then dropped to his knees without a backward look, scrambled to his cell and put a big flat stone over the hole, lest the long-haired one should follow and kill him. As for the girl, seeing the swift-running lad, she watched in surprise for a little, then followed, and coming to the hole in the ground shuddered with fear, believing that under the earth she trod lived thousands of such creatures that, perchance, roamed in the daytime and did evil.

The next day when the witch let the lad out after shutting the girl in her stone place, she was surprised to see fear in his eyes, for all that night he had lain awake in his dread of the long-haired one, trembling at every sound, lest the unknown should find the passage and creep through into his cell of safety.

All that day he worked hard, rolling a great boulder up from the valley so that he might close the outer opening of his burrow, but so heavy was the rock and so far the distance, that the sun set before he had rolled it to its place. Still, he moved it a long way and got it over his burrow and close to the bush. Then he sought the witch so that she might lock him up for the night, but to his grief she did not come, and this is why:

After she had unlocked the girl's door that evening she remembered the look of fear that had been in the lad's eyes, so went into his cell to see if anything harmful was there, and her foot struck the flat stone. Then she found the opening of the hole. Wondering greatly, she crawled into the passage, pushing hard because it was too small for her. At one place she had to remove much dirt above her head because the roof was so low, and pulling away a stone, down came a shower of little stones and of earth, then more and still more, until with a thundering noise the big boulder, which the lad had rolled and left, fell into the hole and very narrowly escaped the witch. So she was stuck fast, deep buried in the ground, her onward way blocked by the boulder against which she butted her head in vain. As for getting back by the way she had come, that was impossible, for, finding night coming on and no guardian witch, the boy fled to his cell. There he saw the black, uncovered hole and the flat rock he had placed over it, and listening he heard sounds in the tunnel. In his fear of the long-haired creature he pulled the flat rock over the hole again and on it piled rock upon rock. That done he gave a sigh of relief and straightened himself, but his heart sank when he saw in his cell the very thing that he most dreaded. For the girl, being brave in the dark and glad in the silence, sought a companion in her loneliness, and found the boy's cell with its open door. But with the lad night brought fear. In the golden sunshine he met danger gladly enough, but in the soft moonlight when the true forms of things were lost, the world seemed baseless and dreamlike and unsubstantial. So, seeing the creature of the night in his cell, he threw up his arms and, not daring to look, fled into the garden and into the ghostly world.

The whispering stillness of what he saw made him tremble violently, for it was a dead world and not the world throbbing with the sweet song of friendly birds and the noise of busy insects. The green and gold of day had strangely gone and the brave hardness that he knew in his world was not in the sky, but instead, a soft black roof hung with strange lights. And even his feet were robbed of speed, and trees and bushes clawed him. As he fled he looked over his shoulder in affright because of the long-haired pursuer. Not far did he go before a creeping vine caught him about the ankle and his foot struck a root, so that he fell headlong, striking his head against a tree-trunk. The silver-sprinkled sky whirled wildly and then all went black.

He woke to the touch of delicate light hands bathing his face with cool water, but lay with fast-closed eyes, believing, hoping that it was a dream. Presently, though still faint and weary and in pain, he opened his eyes to see the face of the maiden as she bent over him, and the cloud of soft hair that rippled as silk grass ripples when touched by the breeze. As he looked, finding something gentle and kind in the face, he chanced to see the white moon, great and cold, rushing swiftly through an army of silver clouds. The sight was new and terrible and he grew dizzy and faint. Something evil seemed to have stolen the warmth from the sky so that the birds had died and the flowers withered.

With eyelids closed he wrestled with his fear and heard the golden voice of the girl saying again and again:

"Am I not your friend in this lonely place? Am I not your friend? Why then do you run from me?"

In spite of his fear he was wrapped in happiness at the words, for he knew that he had been long lonely, though he had not told himself so until then. Yet the darkness stretching wide and the stars and the shadows made him chill at heart, though like a true man he strove to master his fear. While he kept his eyes closed it was well enough, but to open them on the sunless world was pain. For all that, he nerved himself to speak.

"Yes. Let us go," he said, "from this world of shadows," and she, thinking that he meant the place of the witch, took his hand and said, "Yes. Let us go, my new-found friend."

He rose to his feet then and said that he was ready, though he covered his eyes with his hand. Then she told him to wait, saying she knew of a hollow place in a tree in which was a flint the old witch had hidden, and the armadillo had told her there was some magic in it, though what that magic power was he did not know, except that it had the power to cut down trees. It would be well, she added, for them to take it with them.

Great was his loneliness while she was away, and though he opened his eyes once, all things were so strange and cold and silent that he closed them again. Once he heard the shrieking voice of the witch-woman under the ground and he wondered why the sound was so muffled. Had she, too, come near to death in the black world? Again he heard the voice of the owl, melancholy and solemn.

But his new-found friend came soon, to his joy, and she gave him the flint and took his hand to lead him, for he dared not open his eyes because of the moon, and she thought him sightless. So all that night they ran thus, hand in hand, over places where there were cruel sharp stones, across mist-blown swamps and pantano lands, and where the way was hard he carried the maiden, though he always kept his eyes closed and trusted to her guidance.

So the girl was strong and helpful to him until the dark began to pass, then, with the rose of dawn the lad cried joyfully, "I fear no more now and am strong again. Perhaps it is the magic of the flint that makes me so."

But she said, "Alas! I fear that the stone we carry is not good but evil. Let us throw it away, for I grow weak and afraid and ill at ease. Greatly I fear the sky so hard and blue, my new-found friend."

Hearing that, he laughed a little and called her his Golden One and bade her trust in him, so she was comforted a little, though still afraid. Then, as the rose and gold of sunrise sped across the sky and the thousand birds awoke and burst into song, his heart was full of happiness, but she, having heard no such noise before, wept with the utter pain of it, clapping her hands over her ears. Her eyes, too, were full of burning pain because of the growing flood of light. Still, she fought with her fear for a while, though she was sadly longing for the world with its friendly dark. But when the sun came up in his brilliancy and the boy greeted it with a great shout of joy, she was as one stunned and said:

"Alas! Go, dear lad, and leave me to die all parched and withered. For into the burning light I cannot go. My eyes are scorched and my brain is on fire. The sweet silence is no more and the heart of night is dead."

At that sad speech the lad was full of grief lest he should lose his new-found friend, so he pulled from the trees light-green branches and wove them into a canopy and bound about her brow a veil of cool greenness, then lifting her in his arms, he went on happy in the singing sunshine, yet sad because she was white-faced and full of strange tremblings. At noon, when the heat of day was like brass and the sky was fierce with light, they came to a place of tender green coolness where was a vine-hung hollow in the mountain side, and there they rested awhile. The lad made for the maid a seat of matted leaves and mosses and brought to her berries and fruits and tender roots, and for drink, cool water in a leaf.

So at last came the light between day and night when neither was afraid, she brave at heart because of the passing

of the burning light of day and he fearless because the night
of sorrow had not yet come. Hand in hand they went towards a great plain all flower-spangled and smiling.

The witch they had forgotten, or thinking of her had supposed her to be fast in her own place. Yet it was not so, for
deep in the burrow in which she had vainly tried to go back
and as vainly tried to go forward she had her mind made up
to escape by some means. With a mighty heave, for she was
of great strength, she burst her way out of the ground and
then stood, shaking the dirt out of her eyes and her ears and
her hair. That done she sought the boy and the girl, but
found no trace of them. At last the armadillo who always tells
secrets, told her of what had happened, so she sought the
magic flint, the terrible cutting flint which she could throw
to kill. Finding it, too, gone, she was in mad rage, whirling,
leaping, and screaming. Another moment and she left the
place, going in mighty leaps, her bow and arrow in her hand,
and soon from the top of a hill she saw the boy and girl as
they stood looking at the smiling valley.

Now that valley was the valley of the huanacos wherein
the witch was powerless, and that she well knew. Did the
two once gain the shelter of the mountains, all her witcheries
would be of no avail. Indeed, that very thing the sentinel
huanaco was telling the children at the very moment the
witch caught sight of them, and the animal bade them haste
lest the witch touch them before they crossed the plain. So
hand in hand boy and girl ran, and seeing them so near
safety the witch went over the ground like a horse, bounding
over bush and stone, taking five yards at each stride.

Then to help the children, from right and from left came
huanacos, by tens and twenties and hundreds, their proud
heads held high, their soft eyes full of loving kindness, and

they ran by the side of the two who fled, and some formed in a body behind them so that the arrows shot by the witch could not touch boy or girl, though many a good huanaco laid down his life, thus shielding them.

Seeing the pass to which things had come, the old witch bethought her of another plan, and taking her magic arrow she shot it high in the air so that it passed over the herd of huanacos and fell to earth far in front of the boy and girl. As soon as the shaft touched the ground it split into a thousand pieces, each no thicker than spider silk, and each fragment took root and became a tree. In a single moment the whole plain was covered with a thick, solemn tangle of forest through which no living creature could hope to pass, and sadly enough, boy and girl turned to behold the witch coming toward them fast. But all about her feet were the animal friends of the boy and girl, foxes and small creatures, while about her head flew many tinamou-partridges, so that soon she was forced to slacken her pace. Then to boy and girl came a puma, smooth and beautiful, and it said, "El pedernal! El pedernal!" and they at once remembered the magic flint.

Taking the stone and poising it the lad threw with all his might. Through the air it hummed, and hearing the music of it the old witch gave a piercing yell, for well she knew its power. Straight toward the forest the stone flew, and before it trees fell to right and left as though the stone had been a great and keen axe handled by a giant, and the path it made was straight and open and clear, so that through the gap they saw the valley. Again the huanacos closed about the boy and girl so that nothing might harm them, and down through the straight opening they all went. Nor was that all. Having cut a way through the forest tangle the flint dropped and buried itself into the ground, boring down and down, until it fell into the lake of clear water that lies hidden under the ground. Out of the hole came bubbling a stream of water, silver and cool, and it flowed down the gap in the forest and passed out on the farther side, then split to run on both sides of the witch, to whom water was death. Deeper and deeper became the water until it covered the very colina on which she stood, and when at last the water touched her feet, she melted as sugar does.

"The stream," said the old woman who told us the tale, "went on and on and became Laguna Viedma, and the forest is the forest you see. As for the boy and the girl, they became man and wife and lived in the place where we now sit for many, many years, and about them stayed many huanacos and deer and tinamou, and the sorry past was soon forgotten like a last year's nest."

Having said all that, the old woman, whose face was wrinkled and brown, drew a white woollen poncho over her shoulders and eyed me. After a while she said that she had told that tale to four men at different times and each of them had liked it so well that he had given her a dollar of silver.

"And," said she with spirit, "I can show you the dollars to prove that what I say is true." So getting up she went into the house and soon came out again with four silver coins, carrying them in her open palm. For a little while she was silent and so was I, and the men sitting around pretended to be inattentive and lit cigarettes and blew smoke rings, jangling their big spurs now and then. Presently the old woman said:

"Some day a brave caballero will hear the tale and he will make the four dollars to be five."

Thinking it well to be counted brave, and hoping that I was a gentleman, I brought her expectations to pass, having a dollar with me, as luck had it. And certainly I think that the tale was worth a dollar, and if it was not, then it was worth many dollars to rest a while in that quiet place and to meet such worthy and simple folk.

THE MAGIC KNOT

THERE was once a lad whose name was Borac who might have been the son of a king, and again might not. No one ever really knew, though a wise old woman who lived near by said that he was, and so many things that she said were found to be true that people believed what she said of Borac. Borac was found by the side of a lake by a man who was gathering fruit. This man saw what he took to be a shining white stone, and, going to it, found a basket neatly made of silk grass lined with soft white feathers, and in it, warm and cosy like a bird in a nest, was the child Borac. So the man took the basket and the baby home with him, and his children were delighted with their new playmate. That made four children for the man and his wife to take care of, for he had three of his own, but good luck came to him from the day he found Borac and things went very well. As for the newcomer, he was treated exactly as were the rest of the children in that house, and like them grew strong of limb and ruddy of face.

So there were two boys and two girls, playmates, and each

day was a golden one for them. Somehow, Borac seemed to see things and to know things that the others often missed. Not that his sight was any better than the sight of his foster-brother and -sisters, for in the place where they lived at the foot of the mountains, where the air was clean and sharp, everyone had good eyesight. Things at a distance were as clear-cut as things are when you look through a field-glass. But as Borac grew, he saw beauty in common things and pointed out to the others the colours in the sunset sky, the pure blue of the lake water, the sun-sparkle on the stream, and the fresh green of the hill grass. Then, too, there were the songs of the birds. That music they had grown up with, had heard so often that they had forgotten the beauty of it all, until one day Borac began to call like a bird and from every tree and bush came a chorus so rich and so wonderful that the joy in their hearts was more like a sweet pain. You know how that is.

Now there was a place in the mountains where the cliff ran straight up, and so smooth it was that no one had ever climbed it, though the children there were sure-footed as goats and could climb the highest places without growing faint or dizzy when high up.

Half-way up this cliff was a broad ledge on which a condor had built its nest, and Borac and his friends often played at the foot of the cliff and loved to watch the condor drop off of his rock shelf with spread wings and float far above, winding in mighty circles for hours, floating higher and higher into the sky without wing motion and just leaning over, it seemed, to go with the wind or against the wind, up and up, until he looked no larger than a humming-bird against the blue. So high he went sometimes that if one but blinked for a moment, the little black spot seemed to disappear. If any one of them had been granted a wish, that wish would have been that he or she might have the power to soar and wheel like the great bird, sweeping up in a great curve to hang in the air, floating downward in a long, long line, sliding, as it were, to sweep up again at will.

One day when Borac and his three friends were there, one of the girls called out in great trouble, pointing up the face of the cliff to a place where was a cranny, and looking, the others saw a large mottled owl with two staring eyes perched on a point of rock, and just below they could make out a pigeon on its nest. It seemed to them that the owl was screaming, "Ah! I see you, little dove. Sharp as needles are my claws. Sharp, too, is my beak to tear you, and little owls are hungry for the flesh of doves."

That seemed very terrible to those who saw, and the four children began to shout and to throw stones, trying to chase the owl away, but it was of no use. The nest of the rock-pigeon was too far away and the face of the rock too smooth and sheer for any of them to climb, so there seemed nothing for it but to watch until the little bird was captured. The pigeon, they saw, was in great fear, but in spite of the danger stayed on the nest. As for the owl, he turned his face downwards toward them, hearing the noise, and they saw his cruel eyes and his head-feathers that were like horns, but he gave no sign of going away. Indeed, he hooted at them, as if to say, "Who cares for you, little earth-creatures?"

To the watchers it was like a jailor hanging over a prisoner who is innocent, or like a man with a sword about to deal a death-blow to a child. It was very sad to them to see the dove all helpless and, above her, the owl ready to dash down at any moment. As for Borac, he was so full of grief that he had started to climb the cliff, though it was clear to him as well as to his friends that he could not mount far. When he had climbed some little way up, a wonderful thing came to pass. From the sky where the condor wheeled, came dropping a long feather, a wing-feather which the great bird had plucked, and it fell spinning and at last rested on a little rock hump close to Borac's right hand. His left hand, meanwhile, was clutching fast to the rock above his head.

Now why Borac should pick up such a thing as a feather when he needed his hands free he did not know, and certainly none of his friends could guess. But he did so, and not only that but looked at it curiously, just as you would do, to note the smooth lines of it and the beauty of the thing. And as he did this he twisted it just a little, gave it a turn with his fingers. At that he floated gently from the face of the rock, out from the cliff and into the air, until he was poised over the heads of his companions, hanging as lightly as a piece of thistle-down. Again he twisted it, just a little, and went upward. Then he tried other things, pointing it a little toward the face of the cliff, and, wonderful enough, floated that way. So he as well as the children knew that there was magic in the feather. Up then he darted with its aid, swiftly as the swiftest bird, rushing through the air, then swooped away from the cliff most beautifully, went upward again, made a great circle as he dived again, then shot upward, and so to the place where the owl sat.

Seeing him, the sharp-clawed thing raised its wings and softly flew away and was seen no more.

Somehow, the three at the foot of the cliff were not at all afraid. They knew everything would come right. Indeed, they leaped with joy and delight when they saw Borac standing on the rock ledge, and they clapped their hands when they heard the little slate-coloured creature coo with gratitude when the owl vanished. But what Borac did next they could not tell, though they saw him stoop and pick up something.

This is what happened: Borac, up there, saw behind the dove's nest a coil of silky stuff no thicker than a fine thread, and in the middle of it was a queer knot. At first he thought it was a part of the nest, so would not touch it, but soon the bird rose from its nest, picked up the end of the thread, and walked with it to Borac. He took it then, wound in the rest of the coil, and it lay in his hand taking up no more room than a wild cherry would, so very fine it was in texture. But he knew at once that he had the magic knot of which the old woman had so often spoken, the magic knot that could bind evil things, though they were so strong that they could lift rocks. How the magic knot got there neither he nor any one else could know, and it did not matter very much. Certainly but for it, the owl would have captured the dove. The condor may have known about it, for condors are very wise, travel far, and see much that escapes the eyes of men. Anyway, Borac did not stay long, but feather in hand leaped into the air, though he was so high that his friends looked to him no larger than foxes, and swooping down landed lightly on the earth.

Then there were experiments. Each of the children wanted to try the feather in turn and great fun they had that evening, flying higher and higher as they grew braver, until at last each of them had stood on the far-away shelf where was the condor's nest. It was easy to do and they found that all would go well so long as there was neither doubt nor fear. The magic feather would carry them quite safely so long as they believed in it. If they did not believe in it, then not a foot could they get from the earth. As for the magic thread with its wonderful knot, what good that might be they did not know, but it was certainly magic, and magic things, as they knew, always come in useful. So they guarded it carefully, packing it away in a nutshell where it should be handy when needed. And the magic knot came in useful much sooner than they expected, and if you are not going to be scared you may hear the tale, but if the hearing of it will make you nervous in the dark, or cause you to be afraid so that at night, being outside the house and nearing it, you make a hurried run to get to the door, then you had better read no farther. For you may as well understand that the magic knot did actually do the work and the thing that it bound is bound for ever and ever, so that no one of you should be afraid of the dark, nor be shivery as your hand is set on the door latch lest something should leap out of the dark and seize you.

Here then is the place to stop if you are timid, but if you are not you may read what comes next and after these three stars:

*   *   *

One night in the village next to that in which Borac and his three friends lived, something happened. In a little house that sat near a clearing some people were sitting talking, and being thirsty one of them asked the boy of the house to take the gourd and go to the stream for water. He did so, going bravely into the dark, for the stream was but a hundred steps away from the house door. The people in the house waited and waited, wondering why the boy was so long, and at last someone went to look for him. Down to the little river they went and back again, but there was no sign of the boy.

Now that was bad enough, but what was worse was that

on the next night a boy went to visit a friend who lived five houses away, and that boy never reached his friend's house. His father and mother went to look for him and traced his footsteps in the sandy road, but came to a place where the steps stopped and beyond was smooth sand. Then on the third night something happened. A girl and her sister were visiting and the younger girl started to go home alone. No sooner had she left than her sister, remembering how the boys had vanished, ran after her to bear her company. The night was moonless and a thin cold mist hid the stars, but the sister could see the little one's white dress a little way ahead. She could not see very plainly because it was so dark, but there was no mistake about it. The fluttering white thing was in front, cloudy looking certainly, but there. Then of a sudden something happened. The white cloud that was a dress had vanished. So the older sister ran to the place and heard a voice calling and the sound seemed to come from above her head. She looked up and saw a flutter of white for an instant, then nothing more. Her sister had vanished exactly as a bubble vanishes.

Because of all that there was terror in the village. In the day the people were nervous enough, but at night there was great fear. No one dared stir out after sunset. Even within doors people sat as if on thorns. Then one night when there was no glimmer of light in the sky, a family sitting in a house heard a great tearing sound as if some giant hand was pulling at the thatched roof. The light in the house went out and those who sat in the room crouched trembling, crowding close to one another, their hearts throbbing. When at last it was quiet again they saw that a ragged hole was in the roof, and on the earth floor there was a mark like the claw of a great bird.

That was all, but there was trouble in the hearts of the people, and soon the news of it all came to Borac. He listened to the tale attentively and so did the wise old woman who was there. She nodded thoughtfully and said:

"But have no fear. Things will not go ill while the moon shines."

She said much more, particularly asking Borac if he had the magic knot, and then she told him what to do. And with the growing moon the trouble ceased.

Meanwhile, Borac was busy. The old woman had talked with him as has been said, and day after day with the help of his magic feather he made great flights, circling high in the sky, crossing valleys, and passing over mountain and lake, and seeing strange lands far to the west and the great ocean that reached far until it touched the sky. Then the condors were good to him and with them he flew hither and thither, as fast and as high as they, never tiring, never lagging, and they took him in a new direction and to a place where out of a great bare valley rose a monstrous black bird, a bird so strong that it could bear away a llama in each claw and another in its beak. So big it was that beside it a condor seemed tiny. It was an ugly bird and the eye of it was heavy-lidded and baleful, its claws sharp. The wings flapped so heavily that the wind from them caused the trees near by to bend their tops as if they leaned to whisper, one to another. Borac at once knew it for the great bird of evil that swooped down on dark nights and carried men away, and he also knew that in the world there was but one and that it laid but one egg.

For many days the lad watched, following the bird wherever it went, and at last discovered it foul nest high up in the mountains where man never set foot. By the side of its nest, in which was an egg so great that a goat might have hidden in the shell of it, was a hole in the rock. In this hole, the sides of which were very steep, were all those whom the great bird had carried away. Day by day, as Borac saw, the bird dropped fruit down into the hole, so that the unhappy creatures might live until the egg was hatched, when they would, he knew, be taken out and given to the young one to eat. When the great bird had flown away, Borac ventured close to the hole and called out to the people there to be of good cheer, for he would rescue them soon and also kill the bird.

Back to his own place he flew then with his magic feather and told everyone what he had seen, and, as the wise old woman advised, Borac and his friends chose a stout tree and cut the top and the branches from it. They then formed the trunk into the shape of a youth, leaving the roots fast in the earth. This figure they painted and covered with a garment and in the hand of it they put a large gourd, so that from afar the thing looked like one going for water. Close to it they built a house of poles and covered it with grass for a roof, in the fashion of the country, and all that they had ready before the moon was again dark. Then everything being prepared, Borac went into the house and waited.

Three nights he was there, then taking his feather flew here and there. At last he saw a great black cloud swiftly moving, which he knew to be the evil bird, so he made for his house and soon there came a great tearing sound in the air. As the bird came it set up a terrific screeching and the noise that it made with the beating of its wings was like thunder-claps. Down it swooped on the man of wood, claws outstretched and beak open, and in another moment it had seized the figure and was trying to lift it. The more the figure resisted, the tighter the evil bird held, its claws and beak fast sunk in the wood. So fearful were its struggles that the earth about the root of the tree heaved, and it seemed as if the roots would be torn out bodily. Then finding that it could not move the thing, the bird made to fly away, but its talons and beak were held by the wood as if in a vise. All its flappings and tearings then were of no avail, and try as it would, it could not release itself. Faster and harder it beat its wings and the wind from them bowed the bushes and shook the house in which Borac was hidden.

Then Borac came forth with magic feather and magic knot, and was soon in the air above the struggling bird. Hovering there he unloosed the thread with the magic knot and lowered it. Down it dropped and was soon entangled in the beating wings like a web about a fly, and, slight though the thread was, against the power of the magic knot nothing could prevail. So in a short time the great black bird was bound for ever.

In the morning Borac flew to the nest in the far valley and went down into the pit in which were the unlucky ones that the bird had caught. One by one he carried them from that place and to their homes. As for the egg, putting his shoulder against it he tumbled it from the ledge where the nest was, and it fell and was smashed to pieces. So there was an end of the evil bird, which soon died; and it was the last of its kind; and to-day, of all the birds of the air, there are none to do harm to man.

THE BAD WISHERS

FOR days and days and for weeks and weeks Canassa and I rode to the south, and the only break in our days was when we changed our tired horses for fresh ones. That we did sometimes four times in the day. We had plenty of choice, for we were driving some three hundred mares and colts. Canassa was a gaucho, a plainsman, as we would say, and a most excellent horseman, so he made nothing at all of catching an unbroken colt with his lasso and saddling and riding it, doing his share of the driving with the horse new to saddle.

With so much of it I grew tired, and one night as we sat about our little campfire heating water for our maté, the tea we made from herbs, I said that I wished the job was at an end.

Canassa strummed his guitar awhile, then laid it aside and said:

"Wishes are no good and he who wishes, risks. For why? Whenever you wish, you leave out something that should not be left out, and so things go wrong."

I told him that a small wish might be all right, but this
he would not allow. Things had to go just so, he said, and
no one in the world was wise enough to wish things as they
should be wished. Then, in the way of the men of the pampas, he told me a tale to prove the truth of what he said,
and this was the tale:

Once there was a woman in Paraguay who had no children and she wished day and night for a boy and a girl.
She did more than wish, going to a place in the woods
where were wild sweet limes and oranges and lemons, and
where the pools were covered with great leaves of water-lilies,
and in the quiet of that place she made a song about the
children she wished for. In that song she sang of the boy
as handsome and swift of foot and strong of arm, and she
sang of the girl as a light creature with keen eyes and silken
hair. Day after day she did this and at last her wish came true,
for she had a boy and a girl and the boy was straight-limbed
and well made and the girl as lovely as a flower of the air.

So far, so good. But that was not the end. The woman
had wished that the boy might be strong and brave and
swift and all these he was. But she had not thought of other
things, and, sad to say, he lacked sight. For him there was
neither day nor night, neither sun nor moon, neither green
of the pampas nor blue of the sky. As for the girl, it is
true that she had sight so keen that she could see the eye of
a humming-bird at a hundred paces, but her legs were
withered and useless and she could not walk, for the mother
in wishing had said nothing of her health and strength. To
crawl about, helping herself with her hands, was as much as
she could do.

Seeing what had come to pass the mother was very sad,

for her dream had become a very pesadilla, a nightmare. So she grieved and each day grew paler, and at last one evening caught her children in her arms and kissed them and they saw her no more, the neighbours next morning telling them that she had died.

Now one day when the children were well grown, there came to the house in which they lived a man in a torn poncho who said that he had walked hundreds of miles, from the land of the Noseless People where it is always cold. He was tired and hungry and torn with thorn-bushes, and his feet were cut with stones. So the boy and girl took him into the house and gave him water to wash himself with and chipa bread made of mandioca flour and sweet raspadura in banana leaves. When he was well rested and refreshed, in return for their great kindness he told them of a strange old witch woman who lived far away, one who knew many secrets by means of which she could do wonderful things.

"In a turn of the hand," said he, "she could make the girl strong of limb and with another turn could restore sight to the lad."

Then he went on to tell of other witches that he knew, saying that there were many who were not all bad, but like men, were a mixture. True, they sometimes kept children, but that was not to be laid to their meanness but rather to their love of beauty. "For," he said, "it is no more wrong to keep a child to look at than it is to pluck a flower or to cage a bird. Or, to put it another way, it is as wrong to cage a bird as it is to steal a child."

The meal being done the three of them sang a little, and the sun being set the old man bade them good-night and stretched out under a tree to sleep, and the next morning before the children awoke he had gone.

All that day brother and sister talked much of what the old man had told them, and the girl's face flushed red and her eyes were bright as she looked at her brother and thought of how sweet it would be if he could see the mists of the morning and the cool cleanness of the night. Meanwhile he in his dark world wondered how he could find his way to the witch and persuade her to work her magic, so that his sister might be able to go up and down, and to skip and dance on limbs that were alive. So at last they fell to talking, and the end of it all was that they started on a journey to the witch, the brother carrying the sister on his shoulder while she guided him safely through thorn-thicket, past swamps where alligators lay hidden, and through valleys where bushy palmetto grew shoulder high. Each night they found some cool place where was a spring of crystal, or a pool of dark sweet water, and at last they came to the little hills where the witch lived.

They found that all was as the old man had said, for the witch was a lonely creature who saw few, because few passed that way. She was glad enough to see her visitors and led them to a fragrant leafy place, and seeing that the girl was drooping like a wind-wearied bird, did what things she could. To the boy she told tales of the birds and the golden light of the sun and the green of spreading branches, thinking that with her tales they would be comforted and content to stay with her in her soft green valley. But the more she did for their comfort and the more she told them of the wonders of the world, the greater was their desire to be whole, the girl with her limbs unbound, the boy with his eyes unsealed.

Before long the lad told the witch of the old man's visit and of their hopes that had led them to take the great journey, and then the old woman's heart fell as she saw her dream of companionship vanish. She knew that as soon as they were whole again they would leave her as the birds that she fed and tended in nesting time left her when winter came. Then she told them no more pleasant tales, but tales of things dead and cold, of gray skies and desert places, of tangled forests where evil things lived.

"It is better not to see at all," she said, "than to see foul things and heart-searing things."

But the boy spoke up and said:

"There being such things, the more I would have my eyesight, so that I might clear those tangled forests of the evil beasts of which you speak."

Hearing that, the witch sighed, though her heart was glad at the boy's words. So she turned to the girl, telling her of the harm that sometimes came to those who walked, of the creatures that do violence and scratch and maul; of stocks and stones that hurt and cut tender feet; of venomous things that hide under rocks. But the girl heard patiently, then clasped her hands and said:

"And that is all the more reason that I ask what I ask, for with feet light and active I can skip away from the hurtful things, if indeed my brother does not kill them."

"Well," said the witch, "perhaps when you know the beauty of the place in which I live, you will be content to stay with me. I must do what you ask because you are what you are by reason of a wish that went wrong. Now to get the magic leaves with which to cure you I must take a journey of a day and a night, and it is part of the magic that those who would be cured must do a task. So to-morrow while I am away you must work, and if I find the task finished you shall be cured. But if you should not finish the task, then all will remain as it is; but I will be eyes for the boy, telling him of the fine things of the world, and for the girl I will be as limbs, running for her, working for her. But I shall do and not wish. Truth is that I would gladly see both of you whole again, but then you would go away, and I sorely lack companionship."

After a little the witch said to the girl:

"Tell me, little one, if this place were yours what would you do to make it better to live in?"

"I would," answered the girl, "have all the thorn-bushes taken away that are now in the little forest behind the house, so that Brother could walk about without being scratched and torn."

"That is fair enough," said the witch. "And you, boy, what would your wish be?"

"I would have all the little stones that are in the valley taken away, so that Sister could play on the soft grass without being hurt."

"Well," said the witch, "it is in the magic that you set your own tasks. So the boy must have every stone cleared away before I return and the girl must see to it that there are no more thorn-bushes. Hard are the things that you have wished."

After the witch had gone there was no joy in the hearts of the children, for it seemed impossible that a blind boy should gather the stones and no more possible for a lame girl to clear the forest. There was a little time in which they tried, but they had to give up. So they stood wondering, and for a moment thought of starting for their own home.

Suddenly, strange to tell, who should come over the hill but the old man in the torn poncho, and they were both very glad to see him. After he had rested awhile they told him their troubles and spoke of their grief because, in spite of all their efforts, it seemed as though all must come to naught.

"I wish——" began the boy, but the old man stopped him with lifted finger.

"Wishing never does," he said. "But help does much and many can help one." He put his fingers to his mouth and gave a peculiar whistle, and at once the sky was darkened with birds and each bird dropped to the ground, picked up a stone and flew away with it, so that the valley was cleared in a moment. He gave another whistle and from everywhere came rabbits which ran into the woods, skipping and leaping, and at once set to work to gnaw the stems of the bushes. And as soon as the bushes fell, foxes came and dragged them away, so that in an hour the forest was clear, and when the witch came back, behold, the set task was done!

So the witch took the leaves that she had brought and made a brew of them, giving the liquid to brother and sister to drink. "But," said she, "see to it that you speak no word, for if you do before sunset, then back you go to your old state."

Both promised that heartily and drank. But as soon as the boy saw the green of the grass, and the blue and crimson and purple flowers, and the humming-birds like living diamonds in the shade, he called out in his great joy:

"Oh, Sister, see how beautiful!" and at once he was in utter darkness again. At the same moment, feeling her limbs strong, the girl was filled with such delight that she tossed her arms into the air and danced. Then from her came a keen cry of pain as she heard her brother's cry and knew that he was blind again. There was a moment when she wanted to lose all that she had gained so that she could tell her brother that she shared his grief, but she remembered that being strong she could help him in his pain, so she went to him and took him by the hand and kissed his cheek.

At sunset the boy, who had been sitting quiet, spoke, turning his sightless face to the witch.

"You have tried to be good to us," he said, "and you have been as kind as it lay in your power to be. Since Sister is well, I am content. And I have seen the beauty of the world, though it was in a flash. So, mother witch, since you have not been able to give us all we ask, we will give you all that we have. Come, then, to the place where we live and see the things that we love, the birds and the flowers and the trees, and we will try in kindness to repay you for what you have done."

Hearing that, the witch suddenly burst into singing and hand-clapping and told them that the spell was broken because she had been befriended.

"No witch am I," she said, "but your own mother who did not die, but was changed to this form for vain wishes."

Then the boy regained his sight and the mother became as she had been, tall and straight and beautiful and kind, and the three of them went to their old home and lived there for many years, very happy and contented.

THE HUNGRY OLD WITCH

SHE was a witch, she was very old, and she was always
hungry, and she lived long ago near a forest where now
is Uruguay, and just in the corner where Brazil and Argen-
tina touch. They were the days when mighty beasts moved
in the marshes and when strange creatures with wings like
bats flew in the air. There were also great worms then, so
strong that they bored through mountains and rocks as an
ordinary worm makes its way through clay. The size and
the strength of the old witch may be guessed when you know
that she once caught one of the giant worms and killed it
for the sake of the stone in its head. And there is this about
the stone—it is green in colour and shaped like an arrow-
head a little blunted, and precious for those who know the
secret, because he who has one may fly through the air between sunrise and sunset, but never in the night.

The old witch had another secret thing. It was a powder,
and the knowledge of how to make it was hers alone and is
now lost. All that is known of it is that it was made from
the dried bodies of tree-frogs mixed with goat's milk. With

it she could, by sprinkling a little of it where wanted, make things grow wonderfully. She could also turn plants to animals with it, or change vines into serpents, thorn-bushes into foxes, little leaves into ants. Living creatures she also changed, turning cats into jaguars, lizards into alligators, and bats into horrible flying things.

This old witch had lived for hundreds of years, so long indeed that the memory of men did not know a time when she was not, and fathers and grandfathers and great grandfathers all had the same tale to tell of how she had always devoured cattle and pigs and goats, making no account at all of carrying off in one night all the animals of a village. To be sure, some had tried to fight her by shooting arrows, but it was of no use, for by her magic the shafts were bent into a shape like a letter V as soon as they touched her. So in time it came about that men would put outside the village in a corral one half of what they had raised in a year, letting the old witch take it, hoping that thus she would leave them in peace.

At last there grew up a lad, a sober fellow of courage, who said little and thought much, and he refused to take animals to the corral when the time came for the old witch to visit that place.

When the people asked him his reason for refusing, he said that he had had a dream in which he saw himself as a bird in a cage, but when he had been there a little while a sweet climbing vine had grown up about the cage and on this vine was a white flower which twisted its way in between the bars. Then, as he looked at it, the flower changed to a smiling maiden who held a golden key in her hand. This key she had given to him and with it he had opened the door of the cage. So, he went on to say, both he and the maiden had gone away. What the end of the dream was he did not know, for at that point he had wakened with the sound of singing and music in his ears, from which he judged that all turned out well, though he had not seen the end of it.

Because of this dream and what it might betoken he said that he would not put anything in the corral for the old witch, but instead would venture forth and seek her out, to the end that the land might be free from her witcheries and evil work. Nor could any persuade him to the contrary.

"It is not right," he said, "that we should give away for nothing that which we have grown and tended and learned to love, nor is it right that we should feed and fatten the evil thing that destroys us."

So the wise men of that place named the lad by a word which means Stout Heart, and because he was loved by all, many trembled and turned pale when the morning came on which he took his lance and alone went off into the forest, ready for whatever might befall.

For three days Stout Heart walked, and at last came to a place all grassy and flowery, where he sat down by the side of a lake under a tree. He was tired, for he had walked far that day and found that slumber began to overtake him. That was well enough, for he was used to sleep under the bare heavens, but with his slumber came confused dreams of harmful things which he seemed to see coming out of the ground, so he climbed into the tree, where he found a resting-place among the branches and was soon asleep.

While he slept there came to the side of the lake the old witch, who cast her basket-net into the water and began to fish, and as she fished she sang in a croaking and harsh voice this:

"Things in the air,
Things in the water—
Nothing is fair,
So come to the slaughter."

They were not the words, but that is what the words meant. But unpleasant as was the song, yet it worked a kind of charm, and things came to her, so that her basket-net was filled again and again. The fish she cast into a kind of wicker cage, of which she had several.

Soon the croaking song chased sleep from the eyes of Stout Heart, and looking down he saw the wrinkled crone and the great pile of fish that she had cast on the bank, and his heart was grieved for two things—one that there was such waste of good life, the other that he had left his spear hidden in the grass. He grieved too, a little, because he knew that on account of his long walk he was weak from hunger and thirst. So there seemed little that could be done and he sat very still, trusting that until he was better prepared for action the old witch would not see him.

But all his stillness was of no avail. Looking at the shadow of the tree as it lay upon the surface of the water, she saw the lad's shadow. Then she looked up and saw him. Had she had her magic green stone with her, things would have been far different and this tale all the shorter. But not having it and being quite unable to climb trees, she said:

"You are faint and hungry. Come down, come down, good lad, for I have much here that is good to eat."

Hearing that, Stout Heart laughed, knowing that she was not to be trusted, and he told her that he was very well indeed where he was. So she tried another trick, spreading on the grass fruits and berries, and saying in a wheedling voice:

"Come, son, eat with me. I do not like to eat alone. Here are fresh fruits and here is honey. Come down that I may talk with you and treat you as a son, for I am very lonesome."

But Stout Heart still laughed at her, although, to be sure, he was a lad of great appetite and his hungriness increased in him.

"Have you any other trap set for me?" he asked.

Hearing that, the witch fell into a black and terrible rage, dancing about and gnashing her teeth, frothing at the mouth and hooking her long nails at him like a cat, and the sight of her was very horrible, but the lad kept his heart up and was well content with his place in the tree, the more as he saw her great strength. For in her rage she plucked a great rock the size of a man's body from the earth where it was sunk deep, and cast it at the tree with such force that the tree shook from root to tip.

For a moment the old witch stood with knit brows, then she went on her hands and knees and fell to gathering up blades of grass until she had a little heap. All the time she was cursing and groaning, grumbling and snarling like a cat. When she had gathered enough grass she stood up and began to sprinkle a grayish powder over the grass heap, and as she did this she talked mumblingly, saying:

> "Creep and crawl—creep and crawl!
> Up the tree-trunk, on the branch.
> Creep and crawl—creep and crawl!
> Over leaf and over twig.
> Seek and find the living thing.
> Pinch him, bite him, torture him.
> Creep and crawl—creep and crawl!
> Make him drop like rotting fruit."

So she went on, moving about in a little circle and sprinkling the powder over the grass. Presently the pile of grass
began to move as if it hid some living thing, and soon the
grass blades became smaller, rounded themselves, and turned
brown. Then from them shot out fine hair-like points which
became legs, and so each separate leaf turned to an ant.
To the tree they scurried and up the trunk they swarmed, a
little army marching over every leaf and twig until the green
became brown, and louder and louder the old witch screamed,
waving her arms the while:

> "Creep and crawl—creep and crawl!
> Up the tree-trunk, on the branch.
> Creep and crawl—creep and crawl!"

The nearer to Stout Heart that they came, the louder she
shrieked, leaping about and waving her long-taloned hands as
she ordered:

> "Seek and find the living thing."

Then Stout Heart knew that trouble was brewing indeed,
for against so many enemies there was no fighting. For a time
he avoided them, but for a time only, and that by going
higher and higher in the tree, crawling along the branch that
hung over the lake, but nearer and nearer the ants came, and
louder she bade them to

> "Pinch him, bite him, torture him."

At last there was nothing for it but to drop out of the tree,
for he had been hanging to the end of a branch and the ants
were already swarming over his hands and some running
down his arms. So he let go his hold and went into the lake
with a splash, down out of the sunshine and into the cool

green-blue of the waters. He swam a little, trying to get out of the way before coming up, but had to put his head out soon to get a breath. Then suddenly he seemed to be in the middle of something that was moving about strangely, and it was with a sudden leaping of the heart that he found himself in the old witch's basket-net being drawn ashore. To be sure, he struggled and tried to escape, but it was of no use. What with her magic and her strength he was no more in her hands than is a little fish in the hands of a man. He was all mixed up with other lake things, with fish and with scum, with water-beetles and sticky weed, with mud and with wriggling creatures, and presently he found himself toppled head foremost into a basket, all dazed and weak. It was dark there, but by the bumping he knew that he was being carried somewhere.

Soon he was tumbled into an evil-smelling place and must have fallen into a trance, or slept. Again, he may not have known what passed because of the old witch's enchantments, for when he came to himself he did not know whether he had been there for a long time or a little. But soon he made out that he was in a stone house and through a small hole in the wall saw that the place where the house stood was bare of grass and full of great gray rocks, and he remembered his dream and thought that it was all very unlike what had really happened.

But in that he was not altogether right, for while he was in no cage and no twining vine with glorious flower was there, yet there was something else. For after a little while a door opened, and he saw standing in a light that nearly blinded him with its brightness a maiden full of winning grace, and light and slender, who stretched out her hand to him and led him out of the dark into a great hall of stone with a vast fireplace. Then having heard his story, which brought tears to her blue eyes, she opened a lattice and showed him a little room where he might hide.

"For," said she, "I also was brought to this place long ago, and when I came the old witch killed one who was her slave before me. But before she died she told me the story of the green stone which the witch has, and also how were used the magic powders. Since then I have been here alone and have been her slave. But now she will kill me and will keep you for her servant until she tires of you, when she will catch another. And so it has been for many, many years, and each one that dies has told the power of the green stone to the other, though none had dared to use it."

Now hearing all that, Stout Heart was all for running away at once and taking the maiden from that dreadful place, but just as he opened his mouth to speak there came to their ears the voice of the old witch.

"Hide then," said the maiden, "and all may yet go well. For I must go to get the green stone by means of which we may fly. With you I will dare. Alone I was afraid to venture."

Even then he hesitated and did not wish to hide, but she thrust him into a little room and closed the door. Through the wall he heard the witch enter and throw a pile of wood on the hearth.

"I have a new prize," said the ogress. "You I have fattened long enough and now you must be my meal. One slave at a time is enough for me, and the lad will do. Go then, fetch pepper and salt, red pepper and black, and see to it that you lose no time, for I am hungry and cannot wait."

The girl went into another room and the witch fell on her knees and began to build a roaring fire. Soon the maiden reëntered, but running lightly, and as she passed the old woman she cast on her some of the magic powder which she had brought instead of salt and pepper. The hag had no idea that it was the powder that the girl had thrown, and thinking that she had been careless with the salt and pepper began to scold her, then getting to her feet took her by the hair, opened the door of the little room in which Stout Heart was, and little knowing that the lad was there cast her in, screaming:

"Stay there, useless one, until I am ready to roast you."

The maiden thrust the green stone into the hands of Stout Heart and at once they flew through the window and out under the arch of the sky. As for the old witch, the powder did its work and she began to swell so that she could not pass out of any of the doors. But presently the boy and girl, from a height at which they could see below them the narrow valley and the witch house, saw that the old hag was struggling to get out by way of the roof.

The two lost no time then. They flew swift and high. But swift too was the witch. Her growing had finished and out over the top of the house she burst, and seeing the escaping pair, began to run in the direction they had taken.

So there was much speeding both in the air and on the earth, and unlucky it was for the two that the green stone allowed those who carried it to fly only in the daytime. All this the maiden told Stout Heart as they flew. The old witch well remembered that at night there was no power in the flying stone and was gleeful in her wicked old heart as she watched the sun and the lengthening shadows. So she kept on with giant strides and leapings, and going at such a rate that she was always very nigh under the two in the air. No deer, no huanaco could have bounded lighter over the ground than she did, and no ostrich could have moved swifter.

When the sun began to drop in the western sky, and he and she were looking at one another with concern as they flew, the maiden bethought her of a plan, and scattering some of the magic powder on the earth she rejoiced to see that the leaves on which the powder fell turned into rabbits. The sight of that the witch could not resist, and she stopped a moment to catch some of the little animals and swallow them, so a little time was won for the fliers.

But the hungry old witch soon went on and regained the time she had lost and was under them again, running as fast as ever. So more powder was scattered, this time on some thorn-bushes, which changed to foxes. Again the old woman stopped to eat and the two gained a little. But the sun was lower and they found themselves dropping ever nearer to the earth, flying indeed but little higher than the tree-tops, and as they saw, the old witch in her leaps lacked but little of touching them.

Ahead of them was the lake in which Stout Heart had been caught, the waters red as blood with the light of the western sky, but the power of the stone was failing with the waning day, and of the powder they had but a small handful left. As for the witch, so near was she that they could hear her breathing, could almost imagine that they felt her terrible claws in their garments.

On the bank of the lake the last handful of the magic powder was cast, and they saw the grass turn to ants and the stones to great turtles as they passed over the water, but so low that their feet almost touched the surface of the lake. The power of the stone was growing weak.

The old witch, seeing the turtles, stopped to swallow them,

shells and heads, and that gave the youth and maiden time enough to reach the opposite shore, where the power of the stone was quite exhausted as the sun touched the rim of the earth. The gentle maiden clung to Stout Heart in great fear then as they saw the old witch plunge into the lake, for she could travel on water as fast as she could on land. Indeed, the fearful old woman cut through the waters so swiftly that a great wave leaped up on either side of her, and it was clear that before the sun had gone she would have her claws in the two friends.

But when she was in the middle of the lake the weight of the turtles she had swallowed began to bear her down. In vain she struggled, making a great uproar and lashing her hands and feet so furiously that the water became hot and a great steam rose up. Her force was spent and the turtles were like great stones within her, so she sank beneath the water, and was seen no more.

Great was the joy of the people when Stout Heart brought the maiden to his home, for she became his wife and was loved by all there as the fairest woman among them.

THE WONDERFUL MIRROR

THIS is the tale of Suso who was the daughter of a very rich man, a very kind-hearted one, too. Never was beggar turned from his door, nor in the length and breadth of his land was there hunger or want. And he loved Suso no less than she loved him. She was very close to his heart and all that could be done to make her happy he did. As for her, there was no pleasure in her day if she was not assured of his happiness.

When her sister had left home to be married, Suso and her father had gone about planning a great park which Suso was to have for her own, a park of terraced, flowered hills. And when it was finished, both birds and animals came to live there and the air was full of song. So in that place Suso played with her companions, and their hearts were in tune with the beauty all about. It was a never-ending pleasure to seek out new places in the great park, cool nooks in which were little waterfalls whose silver music mingled with the whispering of the leaves, or shaded spots where were ponds of crystal water and fountains and seats and bright green carpets of moss.

For a long time there was happiness, until, indeed, her father married again, for her mother had died when Suso was a small child. Then one day there was a cloud of grief in the maiden's heart, because on a silent, moonlit night she had walked with her father and he had told her that he was troubled with a wasting sickness and feared that he had not long to live. Some enemy, he said, had cast a spell on him, so that day by day he grew weaker and weaker and weaker. Wise men and doctors had looked into the matter, had sat solemnly and thought, had guessed and wondered, but had agreed on one thing only—that something was wrong. What that something was they did not know, but they agreed that if the thing that was wrong could be discovered and removed, all would go well again. Because of what her father had told her, Suso was sad and often wandered to a quiet place where she could tell her troubles to the trees.

The stepmother was not at all fair in her ways and not only disliked Suso, but was very mean and treacherous, hiding her hatred from the father and petting Suso when he was near, stroking her hair and saying pretty things. So well did the wicked woman play her part that nothing could have made the father believe other than that she loved Suso quite as much as he did. For instance, on that moonlit night when he had told his daughter of his trouble, seeing her tears, for she had wept bitterly, he had said:

"But Suso, my dove, your mother will care for you tenderly when I am dead, for she loves you dearly."

At that the girl stifled her sobs and dried her tears, lest the father she loved so well should be wounded by her grief, and seeing her calmed he had supposed that all was well and that his words had soothed her.

But see how it really was with Suso and her stepmother. There was one day, not long after, when father and stepmother and daughter were standing by the fountain, watching the wavering shadows flying across the green, when the man suddenly felt a clutching pain at his heart and was forced to sit down for very weakness. When he felt a little better and the first sharpness of the pain had gone, Suso walked with him to the house, and when he was comfortably seated and had a feather robe cast about him, he bade her return to her stepmother. That she did, because she was bid, although her wish would have been to sit at his feet. Because of her unwillingness and her grief she went softly, and not singing and dancing, as was her fashion. And what was her terror when she saw and heard the wicked woman talking to a great horned owl that sat in the hollow of an old tree! So terrible that seemed, that Suso could find nothing to say, but stood with clasped hands, her heart a-flutter. Seeing Suso, the woman motioned to the owl and the bird said no more, but sat listening, its head on one side. Then the stepmother took Suso by the hand and drew her into a place where they could be seen by the father, but far enough away to be out of earshot. But the father, seeing the woman and the maiden standing thus together, was happy, thinking that his daughter had a friend. It made him happier still to see the woman take Suso's arm and pull it gently about her waist. But he did not hear what was said, for had he heard, it would have cut him to the heart.

This is what the woman said, and her voice was like a poison-dart as she whispered loud enough for the owl to hear:

"Suso, stand thus with your arm about my waist so that your father may see us together. Thus he will think that I love you." Then she hissed in the girl's ear: "But I hate you, hate you, hate you."

And the owl lifted his head, blew a little and repeated softly: "Hate you—Hoo!—Hoo!"

From far off in the woods came the sound of an answering owl like an echo: "Hate you—Hoo!—Hoo!" and it seemed to Suso that all the world hated her for no cause, for the screeching parrots, too, repeated the cry. As for the sweet feathered things that she loved, they had all fled from that place.

Soon the stepmother spoke again and the owl dropped to a lower branch the better to hear. "Suso," said the woman, "your father cannot live much longer. The spell is upon him and day by day he nears his death. Because of that I am glad, for when he dies, all this land, the house, and all its riches, must be mine."

Hearing that vicious speech Suso was well nigh faint with fear and horror and would have sped to her father to warn him. But the woman caught her by the wrist, twisting it painfully, and pinched the soft place on her arm with her other hand, and stooping again so that it seemed to the watching father that she kissed Suso, she said:

"But see to it that you say no word, for the moment that you say anything but good of me, that moment your father will fall dead."

So what was Suso to do?

Thus it was that Suso crept to quiet places and told her tale to the whispering leaves and to the evening breeze, and thus it was that in the midst of all that beauty of golden sunlight and silver-glinted waters and flower-twined forest she could not but be sad. For there were tears in her heart, and everything that her father did for her was as nothing and like a crumbling tower.

But she had told the trees (and trees bend their tops though they are foot-fast, and leaves, too, whisper one to another), so that the tale went abroad, though of this, Suso knew nothing.

II

Now while all this was going on there lived in the hills far off a youth, and his name was Huathia. Brown-haired he was and bright-eyed too, with clear skin and strong arms, and all who knew him said that he was a good lad and honest.

He was a herder of goats and llamas, and one day, as he was out in the vega with his flock, he chanced to see a falcon wheeling high in the air, carrying something in its beak that sent the rays of the sun flashing far, like silver light. Then the bird dipped with the thing it was carrying, looking like a glittering falling star, and Huathia for a moment lost sight of the bird as it dropped behind a bush. But it soon rose and took to flight, this time without the shining thing. So Huathia went to the place where the falcon had dropped, and there at the bottom of a little stream he saw a bright round piece of silver. The lad rescued it and looked at it with astonishment as it lay in his hand, a polished and smooth disc it was, that reflected his face as clearly as a mirror. So he kept it, wrapping it in a leaf, and took it that night to the place where the lad lived with another herdsman, a very wise and good man who knew many strange things, and he told the youth that it was the wonderful mirror of one called Paracaca, long since dead. He said that whoever looked in it saw his own face as others saw it, but the owner of the mirror saw something else, "for," added he, "with it you may see the hidden spirit of other people, seeing through the mask they wear. And if a man has the face of a man but the heart of a fox then certainly while such a man beholds his own face, you shall see the other creature in him."

Hearing that, the youth Huathia was much amazed at the magic of the thing and, holding it so that the face of his herder friend was shown in the mirror, saw, not the rough bearded face of the man alone, all knotted like a tree-trunk, but a face that was full of kindness and gentleness, at which he was glad.

So he placed the wonderful mirror in his bag and carried it about with him. The next day, while he was leaning against the trunk of a tree and playing on his flute, he seemed to hear a whispering, and putting his reed away he listened intently. Still and small, still and small were the voices that he heard, as tree-head bent to tree-head and leaf murmured to leaf, but soon he caught the rumour that ran, and learned the tale that in the country of the rich man there was a creature timorous and frail, whose gentle heart was heavy with sorrow, and that an unknown evil brooded dark.

No time lost he then, seeing that there was something of worth that he could possibly do, but gave the care of the goats and llamas to his friend, took his arrows and bow, his bag with a little food and the wonderful mirror, and after bidding his friend good-bye set off for the land of the rich man. What was strange was that while all had been silent in the soft green woods that morning, except for the sound of his flute, no sooner had he started on his way than a gay chorus came from the bright birds and the world was full of mirth. So, well content, he went on his way, a ragged herdsman, but light of heart and strong of limb and brave.

Into the land of the rich man he went and came in time to a place where sat the maiden under a tree, doves at her feet and glittering humming-birds about her head. When Suso saw the youth her heart leaped for joy, for she knew him for a kind lad, though never before had she set eyes on him.

"Are you a beggar and poor?" she asked. "For here there is plenty for all."

"I am no beggar," he answered, "and for myself I am well content with what I have. But it has been whispered about the world and I have heard the tale, that there is a great sorrow upon you, and that some unknown evil is destroying the beauty and the bliss of this place, so I have come to do what is to be done."

At that Suso said no more but rose up and took Huathia by the hand and led him to her father. It was a day on which the good man was very weak, but seeing that his daughter was pleased with her new companion he ordered his servants to spread a table under the trees, and the three of them had a feast of goat's milk and fruit, and cassava bread, though the father could eat but little. Then Huathia took his flute and played sweet music until the world seemed full of peace, and gripping grief had vanished. Suso, too, sang sweetly, so that for a moment the father thought that the shadow that was upon him was but a dream and might pass.

They talked long and long, the three of them, and Huathia learned much about the rich man's failing strength, whereupon it came to him somehow, that by means of his wonderful mirror he might perchance discover what evil thing was about that place. To him the rich man said:

"If with this mirror you can find the hidden evil thing and can restore my strength again, then there is nothing too great that I own which may not be yours for the asking."

"There is but one thing I want," said Huathia. "For I love Suso the gentle and would marry her."

The rich man thought long after this speech, stroking the hair of Suso who sat at his knee, for it had not entered into his mind that his daughter might be the gift which the youth demanded as his price. But looking at the maiden he saw that her eyes were cast down, though for a moment they had looked up swiftly as Huathia spoke. Then, too, it was certain that since the youth had been there, the song of the birds was louder in the thicket and the green of the trees brighter.

So the father said thoughtfully: "If you find the cause of the trouble that is upon me and relieve it so that I am healed again, then you may have my daughter for your wife, though you must promise me that you will stay in this place."

That, Huathia promised readily enough, and stooped to Suso and kissed her, and having done so, went away to the dark pool in the woods to sleep, at the very moment the stepmother came out of the house to join her husband and his daughter.

III

As it happened that night, there was a thin new moon, and the youth slept but little because of the croaking noise made by the frogs. Presently, full awake, he sat up, and it seemed to him that the air was full of noise, not only of frogs but of the hooting of owls and the whirring of bats, and looking he saw the strange sight of a great white toad with two heads, and presently about that fearful thing other things gathered. From rock and hole came unclean crea-

tures, abominable serpents and centipedes and great gray
spiders, and all these gathered in a circle, the two-headed
toad in the centre. With wide-open eyes Huathia watched,
although the sight of so much that was noisome came near
to benumbing and stupefying him, and incomplete shapes
seemed to be looking at him with evil eyes from the black
depth of the forest.

Soon the owl began to mourn and the song fell into words
and the youth heard this:

"Who knows where hides our queen? Hoo! Hoo!"

And first one creature and then another answered:

"The toad, our queen, lies hid unsought
Beneath the stone that men have wrought."

And so it went on, a mad and horrible concert, with bat
and owl and great ghost-moth whirling about on silent wings,
until sickened of it all Huathia rose up and clapping his
hands to his ears fled from the place. And when he had
gained a quiet and lonely spot he sat down, but in his ears
rang what he had heard:

"The toad, our queen, lies hid unsought
Beneath the stone that men have wrought."

So he wondered and wondered where could be the stone
that men had wrought, and the story that men had told of
a great temple on the mountains came to him. But that place
seemed too far away.

When it was full day the youth went to the house, and in
time the rich man came forth and greeted him. Then came
the stepmother, who fixed her large dark eyes on Huathia,
not looking at him straight, but sideways. Suso came shortly
afterward and the youth could not take his eyes from her. It
seemed to him that she was the most beautiful of living
things as she sat on her stool by the side of her father, her

hair touched by the golden light so that it seemed to be as full of ripples as a sun-kissed brook. So there was pleasant talk while they ate, and, after, a drinking-in of soft music as Huathia played on his flute. Suso sang when Huathia had finished, and though her song had a touch of sadness in it, it seemed to her pleased father that all on earth that was soft and shapely and fair was gathered there in that garden, until catching the eye of his wife he was reminded that his life was flowing away, and the old grief came upon him.

Somehow talk fell upon Huathia and his mirror and the strange way in which he had found it, and he took it from his bag. As he looked in it, Suso came and stood behind him, so that he saw the reflection of her face and the true picture of herself, and there was a gentleness there, the gentleness of the dove and the purity of the flower. The rich man came, too, looking over Huathia's shoulder and saw his own reflection. But what the youth saw was a face that denoted great bravery and kindness. Seeing all this the stepmother stretched her hand across the table and took the mirror, gazing at the picture of her own dark beauty. Then Huathia stepped to her side and looked into the disc. He saw, not the dark eyes and night-black hair that she saw, not the face of a proud woman, but the face of a toad, and when she held the polished silver further off, the better to see, the toad-face changed, so that he saw a double-headed toad. But of that she knew nothing and did not even guess that he knew her for a vile witch and no true woman. And as she continued to gaze and her thoughts wandered, so did new things come into the picture that Huathia saw, and he beheld about her neck two writhing white snakes, a sight so horrible that he could scarcely hold his countenance or prevent himself from calling out. Having seen to her content, the woman rose from her stool and left the room.

The rich man, already tired, for his night's sleep did not revive him, stood up and beckoned to the youth to give him an arm. Suso supported him on the other side and so they walked slowly to a seat beneath a great flowering bush near the house. Having found his seat and being wrapped in his feather mantle by Suso, he asked the youth to play the flute again. Huathia was ready and willing, but somehow the memory of the two-headed toad and the two white snakes made him nervous, and when he put his flute to his lips no sweet sounds came, but instead rude noises like the hissing of snakes and the croaking of frogs and screeching of parrots. Even Suso stopped her ears and her father bade the youth cease his noise.

"Are you of those who make my last days the wearier with your noises?" he asked sorrowfully. Then he added: "For many nights I have dreamed of toads with two heads and of snakes that hung over me, and now you come with your flute and the noises that such evil things make. I had expected better of you, Huathia, seeing that I have treated you as a son."

Huathia earnestly assured him that he had no wish to do other than to make music, and he ended by saying: "There is, I am sure, some enchantment in this place, for though the sun is warm I feel a chill, as if some clammy thing enfolded me."

He shivered as he spoke, though he was a lad whose blood ran warm; not afraid, not given to idle fancies. Of a sudden his eyes fell upon a large grindstone that lay near by. It was a stone so great that two men could hardly make shift to raise it, and so it had been left there for years and grasses had grown about it. But when Huathia saw it, there leaped into his mind the song that he had heard:

"The toad, our queen, lies hid unsought
      Beneath the stone that men have wrought."

It had meant little in the night, but in a flash he saw that
the grindstone was a stone wrought by men. So fitting an
arrow to his bow he handed the weapon to Suso, telling her
to shoot whatever evil thing was discovered when he lifted
the stone. With a great effort he raised the stone suddenly,
heavy though it was, lifting it high above his head, and there,
in a hollow place where the stone had been, sat a large, white,
double-headed toad.

"Shoot, Suso, shoot!" commanded the father. "Let not that
evil thing escape. It is the creature that torments me at night."

Swift flew the arrow and it pierced the body of the toad.
At the same moment there fell from the roof of the house
two monstrous white serpents where they had lain hidden.
Like lightning Huathia, having seized the bow, sent two arrows flying, and each serpent was cut into halves. In less
than three moments three evil things died, and it was like
the sun coming from a cloud-veil, the way in which joy came
to that place. The weakness of the father fell from him like
a cloak. The bodies of the toad and the snakes withered and
shrivelled, and as a light breeze sprang up, what was left of
them was blown away as dust. There were soft stirrings in the
thicket and the whole world burst into song. So both father
and daughter knew then that the witcheries were gone and
the evil creatures vanished for ever, and that all the trouble
that had been upon that place came from the wicked stepmother.

So youth and maiden were married, and the father soon
regained his health and strength, and in all the world there
were no happier people than they.

THE TALE OF THE LAZY PEOPLE

IN COLOMBIA, it seems, there were always monkeys, or if not always, at least as far as the memory of man goes. An old historian named Oviedo noted that and wrote: "When the Christians make an expedition to the interior and have to pass by woods, they ought to cover themselves well with their bucklers . . . for the monkeys throw down nuts and branches at them. . . . I knew one, a servant. This man threw a stone at a monkey, who caught it and returned it with such force that it knocked out four or five of Francisco's teeth, and I know this to be true for I often saw the said Francisco, always without his teeth."

Now one day a man told me the tale of the monkeys, and he talked and talked as he smoked, until the stars came out and shone clear and steady and the air was heavy with perfume, and owls and bats floated strangely, as they will do, and when he had finished he still talked, taking up forgotten ends of his tale and winding in and about, making a long affair of a short matter. But then he had nothing else to do but to talk and was mighty pleased, it seemed, to have

someone to listen to him. Then, when we should have been
sleeping, he went on talking, picking out a piece of the tale
here and another piece there, and explaining until I was well
nigh like to get the story tangled myself. But here is the
meat of it:

Long, long ago there were no monkeys, and the trees were
so full of fruit, and the vines of grapes, that the people
became lazy, and at last did little but eat and sleep, being
too idle to carry away the rinds and skins of the fruit that
they lived on, and certainly too lazy to clean their thatched
houses.

It was very pleasant at first, but soon not so pleasant, for
winged things that bit and stung came in thousands to feed
on the things thrown aside, and they, too, grew lazy, finding
so much to eat ready at hand, and when people tried to brush
them away there was a loud and angry buzz and much irri-
tated stinging, so that soon every one was wonder-struck, not
knowing exactly what to do. For a time it seemed easier to
move the little village to a new spot and to build new houses,
for the dwellings were light affairs and in a day or less a
good house could be built. But then they lived by a lake
from which the water for drinking was taken, and as it was
but a little body of water, it was not long before the people
had built right round the still pool and so were back again
at the starting place. As for the stinging flies, they were soon
worse than the mosquitoes, while a great wasp with pink head
and legs and bands of black and gold on its body, though
very pretty to see, was worst of all. So it was no easy matter
to know what to do, and there was much talk and much ar-
gument, and all that the people agreed on was that something had to be done, and that, very soon.

One day there came to the village a queer and rather

faded kind of man, ragged and tattered and torn as though he had scrambled for miles through the thorn-bush forest. He had rough yellow hair, and queer wrinkles at the corners of his eyes which made him look as if he were smiling. It was late in the afternoon when he came and the people were taking their rest after the noon meal, so no one took much notice of him although he went here and there, looking at things, and so walked round the lake. But the curiosity of everyone was excited when he was seen to make a basket, which he did quickly, and then commence to gather up the fruit skins and rinds in one place. Now and then some one or other raised himself in his hammock, with a mind to talk to him, but it seemed almost too much trouble, and when some great blue-winged butterfly fluttered past or some golden-throated humming-bird flashed in the sunlight, their eyes wandered away from the old man and they forgot him again. So the sunlight died and the forest was a velvet blackness and everyone slept, though the old man still worked on, and the next morning when the people awoke he was still working diligently, though he had but a small place cleared after all.

The very thought that any one would work all night made the head man shiver with a kind of excitement, yet he was very curious to know why the stranger went to so much trouble, seeing that he neither lived there nor was of the lake men. At the same time it made his spirit droop to think that if the place was to be cleared up, he and everyone else had a mountain of work in sight. So Tera, the head man, called to Cuco, who was his servant, telling him to bring the stranger to him, and Cuco, who was very respectful, said that he would attend to it. Then Cuco did his part by calling Yana and delivering the message to him. And Yana in turn told his servant, Mata, who told his servant, Pera, who told his servant, Racas, who told a boy, so that at last the message reached the old man. Then back went the old man, handed by the boy to Racas, by Racas to Pera, by Pera to Mata, by Mata to Yana, and by Yana to Cuco, so that at last he stood before Tera, the head man, and the others, being curious to know what was afoot, gathered about.

"What is your name, from where do you come, and what do you want?" asked Tera, putting his three questions at once, to save trouble. Then the head man looked at those about him with a little frown, as much as to say, "Note how wisely I act," and each man who had heard, seeing that the head man looked his way, nodded at his neighbour, as though calling attention to the wisdom of the head man, so all went very well. But the little old man stood there very simply, making no fuss at all and quite unimpressed with the greatness of the great man.

"I want to work," he answered. "I want to be told what you want done and to see that it is done."

To be sure, the language that he spoke was one new to those who listened, but somehow they seemed to understand. But the thing that he said they found truly astonishing and could hardly believe their ears. But the head man, though as astonished as any one there, quickly regained his composure and asked this question:

"What is your trade?"

"I have no trade," said the old man. "But I get things done."

"What kind of things?"

"All kinds of things."

"Do you mean big things, like house-building and all that?" asked the head man.

"Yes. And little things too, which are really big things when you come to consider," said the old man, but that seemed an odd if not a silly thing to say, the head man thought.

"Little things left undone soon become big things," explained the old man, and waved his hand in the direction of a heap of fruit skins and husks near by.

"Yes. Yes. But you must not preach to us, you know," said Tera a little testily. "Tell me the names of the trades you have."

So the little old man began to tell, naming big things and very little things, things important and things not important at all, and having finished, asked very politely whether any one there had anything to be done. As for pay he said that he wanted none at all and would take none, and he said that because some of those gathered about him began offering him things.

For instance, Pera said: "If you work for me, I will let you have one fish out of every ten that you catch, for I am a fisherman." And Racas pushed him aside, saying: "But I will do better, for I am supposed to be fruit gatherer and will give you two things for every ten you gather." And so it went, each bidding higher than his neighbour, until it came to the turn of the man whose duty it was to gather the rinds and fruit skins. He said, "I will let you have, not one out of ten, nor two out of ten, nor five out of ten that you gather, but ten out of ten, if you will work for me." At that the old man said quite positively that he would take no pay at all.

No more was said then and the little old man turned away without as much as bowing to the head man, seeing which the head man waved his hand and said: "You may go, and so that you will lose no time, you need not bow to me." And all the rest gathered there said very hastily: "Nor need you bow to me, either."

The old man took small notice of any one, but went away singing, for he had a gay, light-hearted disposition, and having reached the place he had cleared, he took flat pieces of wood and began cutting out figures like little men, and each figure had a kind of handle that looked like a long tail. Nor did he cease whittling until he had made at least twenty wooden figures for each man in the village. Being finished he stood up to stretch his legs and straighten his back, and when the people asked him what the little figures were for, he shrugged his shoulders but spoke never a word. Then he lifted the figures that he had made, one by one, and set them upright in the sand until there was a long row of them, and took his place in front of them, like a general before his army. It was beautiful to look at, for one figure was as like another as one pin is like another, and for a moment even the old man stood admiring the line. After a moment he waved his hand in a peculiar way, spoke some magic word, and waved his hand again, at which each of the figures came to life and nodded its head, seeing which all the people laughed and clapped their hands. The ragged man bade them make no noise, but watch.

"Since you do not like to work," he said, "I have made twenty figures for each of you, and they will work for you without pay, doing what you require them to do; only observe this, you must not give any figure more than one particular job. And now let each man or woman clap his hands three times, then call out the name of the thing to be done."

When he had said this, the figures started running, twenty gathering in a circle about each man there, bowing from the hips and straightening themselves again, so that their tails of wood went up and down like pump-handles.

"Now see," said the ragged man, "you have things to work for you, and as I call out, the figures will stand forth, each ready to do his task." And he began calling, thus:

"Armadillo hunters, stand forth!" and a hundred and more active figures ran together like soldiers.

So he named others in order as:

Bread makers.

Cassava gatherers.

Despolvadores, who would gather up dust.

Esquiladors, who would shear the goats.

Farsante men, whose work was to amuse tired men.

Guardas, to keep order about the place.

Horneros, or bakers.

Industriosos, who were to do odd jobs everywhere.

Jumentos, whose work it was to carry burdens.

Labradores, to do heavy work and clear away garbage.

Moledores, to grind the corn.

Narradores, who told stories, related gossip and so on.

Olleros, or pot makers.

Pocilga figures, to attend to the pigs.

Queseros, to make cheese from goat's milk.

Rumbosos, or proud-looking things to walk in parades.

Servidores, or food carriers.

Trotadores, to run errands.

Vaqueros, to attend to the cows.

So everyone was well pleased and each one had his twenty figures to do all that needed to be done, and all that day there was a great scraping and cleaning and carrying and currying and hurrying and scurrying. Silently the little figures worked, never stopping, never tiring, never getting in one another's way, and all that the living people had to do was to rest and watch the men of wood, and keep their brains free for higher things. For it must be remembered that before the old man came there with his wonderful gift, the people had complained that there was so much to be done that they had no time to write poems or to make songs or to create music, and that with the daily tasks abolished their brains would be more active.

Not two days had passed before the children of the place complained that they did not have a chance and that they had so much to do, what with hunting for things lost, looking after their small brothers and sisters, keeping things in order, trying to remember things they were told, cleaning things, and a dozen other tasks, that they really had no time to play, much less to study. So they went in a body to the old man and asked him to give each child twenty figures to do odd things. There was a great deal of fire and expression in his eyes when he made answer that if the children really needed help he would lose no time in providing it. But the young people were quite positive that they were overworked, and the long and short of it was that the old man whittled out many, many more figures, and in another twenty-four hours each and every boy and girl had his own

Abaniquero, or fan maker, so that none had to pluck a palm leaf.

Baliquero figure, to carry letters and messages.

Cabrero, to look after the goats.

Desalumbrado, to hunt for things in the dark.

Enseñador, or private teacher, who was never to scold.

Florista, to save them the trouble of gathering flowers.

Guasón figure, to amuse them.

Hojaldarista, whose work it was to make cakes.

Juego figure, to arrange games.
Keeper of things.
Lector, to read and tell stories.
Mimo, to act as clown.
Niñera, to look after younger children.
Obediencia figure, to make others obey.
Postor, to buy things for them.
Quitar figures, to take things away when children tired.
Recordación figures, or rememberers.
Solfeadors, to sing to them.
Tortada men, to make pies.
Volantes, as servants.

So things seemed to be going very well, and before a month had passed in all that place there was not a thing out of order, soiled, broken, bent, lost, misplaced, undone, unclean, or disorderly. Neither man nor woman nor child had to worry; dinners were always prepared, fruits gathered, beds made, houses in perfect order, and all was spick and span. All that the grown-up people had to do was to look on, and no one was proud of the order in his house because every other house in the place was as orderly. As for the children, they had nothing at all to do but to eat, drink, rest, and sleep. Then, presently, more figures were called for as this one or that wanted a larger house, a finer garden, or grander clothes.

But as the wooden figures became more numerous and as no figure could do more than one task, the ragged man had to make figures for the figures and servants for the servants, for as things went on, there had to be more fruit gatherers, more water carriers, more scavengers, more cooks, because the figures had to eat and drink. Thus it came to pass that before long, instead of their being twenty figures for each man, there were sixty or seventy, with new ones coming from the old man's knife every day. Soon the lively manikins were everywhere, inside houses as well as outside, thick as flies in summer and certainly a great deal more persistent, for there could be no closing of doors against the manikins. Indeed, had anything like that been attempted there would have been a great cry for special door-openers. So, many houses were quite cluttered with wooden men, those who were on duty rushing about until it made the head swim to look at them, and those who were resting or sleeping, for soon they learned to rest and to sleep, lying about the floors, piled up in corners, or hanging to rafters by their tails. All that increase in help had made for the production of a thousand or more guardas, whose task it was to keep order, and they were everywhere, alert and watchful and officious, and the real people had to step about very gingerly sometimes, to avoid treading on them and annoying them.

At last there came a day when the people began to grow a little tired of doing nothing, and they told one another that a little help was a very good thing, but help in excess, too much of a good thing altogether. So there was a meeting and much talk and the manikin narradors, whose duty it was to carry gossip and the news, were very busy, rushing from here to there with their scraps of information.

"It is very clear that something must be done," said Tera, the head man.

"But everything *is* being done," answered the little old man. "If *everything* is done, something *must* be done."

"I did not mean that," said Tera, who seemed a little testy. "I meant to say that these wooden men must be kept in their places."

"But they *are* in their places," replied the old man. "Their place is everywhere because they do everything, so they are in their places."

"You see, the days are so very long, so very dull," said the man who wished to have time that he might become a poet. "At the shut of day we are not weary."

"We do not want to be petted," said another.

"The trouble is," sighed a fat man, "you can't be happy when everything is done for you."

"And we don't want to be nobodies," shouted another.

Another said very mournfully: "It seems to me that when these wooden things do things with our things, then the things that they do and make and care for are not our things."

"Too many 'things' in that speech," said the fat man.

"Well, there are too many things," answered the other. "Look at me. I used to be gardener and now I'm nothing. When my garden is dug and planted and tended and watered and the very flowers plucked by these wooden things, and when other wooden things pick up the leaves and pull the weeds and do everything, then my garden does not seem to be mine." He added after awhile: "I hope you know what I mean, because it is not very clear to me, yet it is so. I remember——"

At that the little old man put up his hand and said: "But that is against the contract. You must not try to remember, really you must not, because there are manikins to do all the remembering, if you please."

"Well, but I think——" began the man, when he was again interrupted.

"Please do not think," said the little old man. "We have things to do the thinking, if you please." He thought for a moment, his bent forefinger on his lips, then he said: "I'll see what can be done. It is clear that you are not satisfied, al-

though you have everything that you asked for and certainly
all the time that you want."

"Let us do something," murmured Tera.

"I'm afraid there is nothing that you can do," said the little
old man, "because, as you see, everything is done, and when
everything is done it is quite clear that something cannot be
left to be done. The only thing that is clear is that there is
nothing to be done."

At that the meeting broke up and each went to his own
hammock to think things over, and soon the general cry was:
"We must have elbow room." And hearing that, the little old
man went to work and whittled more figures of wood, a whole
army of them, ten for each living man, woman, and child,
and in voices that creaked like wooden machinery they
marched hither and thither, crying: "Elbow room. Elbow
room!"

Soon there was confusion. It was manikin against manikin
for a time, the Elbow-room-ers thrusting and pushing the other
working manikins, some going about their work with frantic
haste, others interfering with them, clutching at them and at
the things they carried, a tangled knot of them sometimes
staggering, to go down with a crash. Soon in every house was
a jangling tumult, manikins and men running about in houses
and dashing out into the open spaces outside; the noise of
slamming doors and breaking pots; the clamour of animals.
Above all could be heard everywhere cries of "We want elbow room! We want elbow room!" Soon men were running
away from the houses with those strange swift manikins hanging to them sometimes beating them, while other manikins
threw things out of the doors and through windows, food and
household things. And excited children fled too, while their
manikins ran at their sides, some chattering, some acting the

clown as was their duty, some telling stories as they ran, while other strange little figures of wood ran bearing heavy burdens. It was all a dreadful mix-up with no one knowing what to do, no one knowing where to go, and everywhere the manikins who were guardas, or order keepers, ran about, tripping people and manikins alike in the effort to stop the rush. But when the day was near its end there were no people in the houses and the hammocks swung idly, for all the men and women and children, even the white-haired grandfathers and grandmothers, had fled to the further side of the lake, where they could have elbow room, leaving the houses and all that was in them to the manikins.

The next day, the people plucked their fruit for themselves and it seemed as though fruit was never sweeter. The water that they carried from the lake tasted better and cooler than water had for many a long day, and when night came they were happily tired and slept well, without any manikin to swing their hammocks and sing to them. And in the morning they woke early to discover the pink and gold of the sunrise most wonderful to see, and there was music in the sound of the wind among the grasses. So as the day passed they were both amazed and astonished at the wonderful and beautiful things that they had almost forgotten, the sight of butterflies fluttering from flower to flower, the shadows chasing across the hills, the richness of the green earth and the blueness of the sky, the gold of sunlight on the leaves, the rippling water and the bending trees; indeed the memory of the manikin days was like a fearful nightmare. Very light-hearted then they grew and the world was full of the music of their laughter and song, and briskly they worked, enjoying it all, building new houses and making things to put in them.

Meanwhile in the village things had gone queerly. For

one thing the Elbow-room-ers kept up their crowding and pushing, so that the manikins trying to work at their old tasks (and there were many who went on just as before) were sadly hindered. There were other figures of wood with nothing to do, since the people they served were gone, and these fell to quarrelling among themselves and grew mischievous. For instance, the pot makers and the pot cleaners fell out, and the pot cleaners started to break the pots so that the pot makers would have more work to do. That meant that the clay gatherers and the clay diggers had to work harder, then because they worked harder, though to be sure all their work meant nothing and was little more than idle bustle, they grew hungrier and wanted more to eat. Because of all that the fruit gatherers had more to do and the water carriers had to work harder and the cassava bread makers had to bake as they had never baked before. That brought the fire builders into it, and of course the wood gatherers also, for they too had to work harder and to eat more, so still more work came on the food bringers. And all the time the Elbow-room-ers rushed about, always in groups of ten, driving and commanding, rushing on workers and sweeping them aside. So everywhere were little figures hurrying one after the other, going to and fro, busy about nothing, quarrelling about nothing, fighting about nothing.

The trouble came when the Elbow-room-ers interfered with the dogs and the cats, the goats and the hens, pushing and hustling them. For the animals, disliking all the disorder and clatter, fell upon the manikins, workers and idlers alike. Seeing that, the household utensils took a hand and the very pots and kettles ran or rolled or fell, spilling hot water over the wooden things with pump-handle tails. The very embers from the fires leaped into the fray. All the while from the

metates in which the corn had been ground came a low
growling, and the growling formed itself into words:

> Day by day you tortured us—
> Grind, grind, grind.

> Holi! Holi!
> Huqui! Huqui!
> Grind, grind, grind.

> Bring to us the torturers—
> Grind, grind, grind.

> Let them feel our power now—
> Grind. *Grind*. GRIND!

So the metates turned and turned, going round and round
without hands, and presently an Elbow-room-er that was
struggling with a corn-grinder stumbled, and both fell
between the grinding stones and in a moment were crushed
to powder. In a flash house utensils and animals learned the
new trick, and in every house manikins were pushed into the
grinding stones. Then sparks began to fly and roofs to catch
on fire and manikins bolted here and there in confusion,
sometimes jamming in doorways, there were so many and all
in such disorder. Then came dazzling, flickering lightning
and a great rain, so that for very safety the manikins fled to
the forest and climbed the trees. And there they have lived
ever since, for they grew hair and became monkeys. But the
remembrance of all that passed stayed with them, and in their
hearts to this very day is no love for man, and for that very
reason when a Christian passes through a forest he must look
well to himself, lest the manikins in revenge try to hurt him
by casting nuts and branches at his head.

THE KILLING OF CABRAKAN

CABRAKAN the giant was slain by the twin brothers and the manner of his killing was thus:

After the death of Cakix and the turning to stone of Zipacna, Cabrakan kept close to the stony land, but one day venturing over the mountains where lived the crag men, he came upon a herd of goats that had wandered out of the way, and gathering them into a corral formed of his legs as he sat upon the ground, he swallowed them one by one, as a child swallows berries. The goatherd saw him from the shelter of a tree, where he hid himself when he first set eyes on Cabrakan. On the next day the giant came again to the same place where he had fared so well, and seeing a house a little way off went there and made a meal of the cattle, leaving the man of the house in sorry case. The third day he ventured farther, sitting down at noon by the side of a village and picking up and eating such living creatures as he chanced to see, much as an ant-eater picks up ants. Nor was there aught to hinder him, for the people fled to the woods when they heard the earth tremble under his tread. So, soon, the tale of how Cabrakan was robbing men came to the ears of the twin brothers, and they swore to stay his high hand forevermore.

Now Cabrakan knew of the manner in which Cakix had been laid low and knew also how Zipacna had met his end, so by neither of these ways was it possible to destroy him. He had also pondered in his slow way, laying half-plans to slay the twin brothers did he ever lay hands on them. Cabrakan was the mightiest of giants and vain of his strength, and in that vanity lay his weakness.

One day there came a mighty storm and a turmoil of wind and water, of thunder and lightning, so that the trees of the forest were laid low and the rocks uprooted, while the thunderings of the sea-waves shook the very barancas. Black were the heavens and clouds flew fast and low, so that Cabrakan in his long life had seen nothing like it, and his heart failed him. Nor did he rise all that day from the shelter of the mountain where he had cast himself on the ground, until the black had changed to gray and the wind was abated. But when the clouds had passed and the sky was again moonlit, he saw on a hilltop a little way off the twin brothers, Hunapu and Balanque. While the storm had raged they were sheltered in a cave, and from it they had seen Cabrakan as he ran before the storm to seek the shelter of the mountain. To their ears, when there were wind lulls, came the sound of mighty whimpering and wailing from the giant, by which they knew that his heart was far from stout.

Seeing the twin brothers, Cabrakan rose to his feet and asked them what they did there, and would have said more had he not suddenly found his mind a blank. So he fell back on his chant, though there was a quaver in his voice because of the fear in him that had not yet died, the fear of the storm:

> "I am Cabrakan,
> Cabrakan who shakes the earth,
> Cabrakan who shakes the sky,
> I am Cabrakan,
> Master of men!"

When he had made an end of his song Hunapu spoke and said, boldly enough: "It is well, Cabrakan. Strong thou art, but so also are we strong. Have you not seen how with our breaths we laid low the trees of the forest? Saw ye not how we blew and the rocks were uprooted? How, also, the skies were darkened? But that was a small matter, for there are things to be done, and in this upsetting of the world my brother alone worked. Now must two of us work, so prepare yourself well, O Cabrakan, lest a giant be blown over the edge of the world where is neither resting-place nor foothold. A trifling matter indeed was the storm."

Hearing that, a deep misgiving was in the heart of Cabrakan. He rubbed his eyes and looked with astonishment at the twin brothers, so slight of build, so ruddy and fair, and seeing them and remembering the storm he could find no words.

Then said Balanque, as had been before agreed between the brothers, and speaking as if in deep thought: "Perhaps it might be better if Cabrakan joined us. It is true that he, the earth-shaker, is after all but weak, but if he be taught to eat of cooked flesh in the manner of men, it may be that he too may grow strong as we are."

Hearing that, the giant pricked up his ears, thinking, in the dull manner of giants, that if he did but play a little to mislead the twin brothers he might persuade them to let him eat of cooked meats, when, his strength becoming greater, he might rid the earth of two who had raised so mighty and fearful a storm. Perchance then, thought he, I shall rule the land alone. So he said, cunningly: "Let me try my strength against yours awhile, and if I be found weak, then cook me the food that men eat, so that I may become strong and thus your useful slave."

At that the twin brothers pretended to consult a little, Hunapu acting as if he wished to raise another whirlwind, Balanque as if soothing him, while Cabrakan stood watching them, a heavy fear in his bones.

"Let Cabrakan," said Hunapu presently, "overturn and pluck out the entrails of this mountain to prove himself." Having so said, he turned aside, but after a moment added, as if his mind had changed on the matter: "Yet how does it matter? We need no Cabrakan to aid us. Perhaps it were better that I cast it over with a breath, even though Cabrakan be blown like a leaf over the edge of the world."

Now though the world in which the giant lived was rocky and bare, yet it looked fair to him and he had no mind to be cast into nothingness. So he made his face fierce and told Hunapu that he was willing to prove his strength. Hunapu, still playing a part, looked scornfully at the giant as he said: "It is after all but a child's matter, but if the mountain be overturned, then shall the food of men be yours and your body made strong and your wits sharpened."

Cabrakan lost no more time but raised his shoulders and put forth his arms as one about to wrestle. "Let none meddle with me," he said, "and before the day breaks I shall pluck out the mountain by its roots." So, a mountain of flesh against the moonlit sky, he strode in five great strides to the side of the mountain and flung his arms about it. First he made a shift to pluck it straight from the earth, his feet set wide apart, his muscles strained and knotted. Again he strove to overturn it, now with shoulder fast-braced against the sheer rock, his legs like towers. That failing, he strove furiously, now battering like a madman, now pressing and stamping, so that there was a trembling all about like an earthquake. So great was his strength that the side of the mountain broke open and a clear stream gushed forth, the water twisting and turning along the plain like a silver snake. All that night and morning he wrestled with the mountain and as the day wore on he grew tired and weary, but there was no result of his labours except the tumbling stream and two great holes in the black living rock at the foot of the mountain where his feet had pushed. But where his arms had encircled, the mountain was worn smooth and bare, the very rock was polished and shone in the sunlight. Grunting and groaning Cabrakan toiled, until at length, seeing that he had grown too weak for mischief, Hunapu called on him to rest awhile.

"Hold thee a little," he said. "This eating of the goats and the cattle of men will make no living thing strong. A heart thou lackest. Like an arrowless quiver or a stringless bow art thou. In the food of men alone is strength, O Cabrakan, so that must we eat, and the meal being done things of worth may be seen."

Well pleased to hear that, the weary giant cast himself down on the ground and rubbed his palms one against another to ease them, but as he lay there resting many a look he gave at the motionless mountain, the glistening head of which he had tried in vain to tear from the sky. Also most heartily he wished that the thing was at an end, or that the twin brothers had stayed away from that place.

Balanque kindled a fire and Hunapu shot an eagle and slowly they roasted the bird, the smell of it pleasing the giant vastly, for he had never tasted cooked meat, nor indeed knew any method of preparing it.

Now in that land there grows a sort of mountain-laurel bearing a red berry within a pod, and its power is such that whoso eats of it will waste away as the morning mist passes before the warming sun. Many of these berries Hunapu took and placed in the flesh of the roasted eagle, for certain it was that neither Balanque nor his brother could leave that place with the giant unslain. So the roasted eagle with the berries in it they gave to Cabrakan, who swallowed it at a single gulp.

At first he felt strong as ten giants and leaped to his feet, minded to pluck the mountain from the earth and cast it on the twin brothers. Fiercely he gripped, so fiercely that the top of the mountain opened and steam came forth and a black smoke rose in the air, spreading in the form of a vast tree; so vast it was, that it formed a cloud that veiled the sun so that the light sickened for a time and a pale yellow touched all things. From the top of the mountain there gushed forth hot lava that glowed as it spread; that came faster soon, in roaring masses. But Cabrakan rapidly waxed weak with the poison of the berries, so weak that he clung for support to the mountain he would have plucked forth. And as his strength waned, the malice within him grew, and dark were the looks, evil the eye he cast on the twin brothers.

But his day was done and his course was run. Soon his eyes grew dim and in very weariness his head fell against the brow of the mountain. Fast and deep for a while came his breath, his chest heaving like a sullen sea when the storm has died. Then his strength fell away altogether and he sank to the earth and the lava covered him.

So came to an end Cabrakan, the earth-shaker and master of men, and thus did the twin brothers finish that which they had set out to do.

THE CAT AND THE DREAM MAN

THIS is a tale that I heard when I was gold digging in Tierra del Fuego, and if you want to get to the tale and skip the introduction, you may. To do that, stop here—and pass over everything until you come to the three stars * * * and begin at "Many years ago." But if you want information and all that kind of thing, read straight on and learn that the man who told me the tale was named Soto, Adolpho Soto. He called himself a Bolivian and said that it was a tale of Bolivia, but he had never been to that country. His parents were Bolivian, but he had been born and reared in inland Patagonia, on the east side of the Cordilleras and north of the great shallow gulf that runs inland from the Strait of Magellan. Anyway, he had heard the tale from others who knew all about the three great stones and how they looked. Certainly he had not read the story, for books meant nothing to him and he would not as much as look at a picture. And it was quite clear to me that he believed every word of the tale. Indeed, I am almost sure that he was doubtful in his mind as to the wisdom of telling me all of it, thinking that I would not believe it. Perhaps that is why he told me the tale in two parts, as if in some manner I might thus get used to the shock of it. Mind you, on the other hand, I am certain that he did not believe all that I told him, though he was too polite to express unbelief. For instance, he could not quite see how carriages went without horses, nor how men sent messages over miles of wire, nor how the sound of a human voice could come from a little box, without magic; for in the country that Adolpho came from there were no railways, no telegraphs, and no phonographs. So to the tale, or rather the first part of it, if you choose to hear it.

*   *   *

The First Part

Many years ago, said Soto, there came into the world a cat. It was in the days when all creatures were harmless; when the teeth and claws of the jaguar did not hurt; when the fang of the serpent was not poisonous; when the very bushes had no thorns. But this cat was of evil heart and unmerciful and a curse to the world, for she went about teaching creatures to scratch and to bite, to tear and to kill, to hide in shady places and leap out on unsuspecting things. Even a sheep she did not leave to its own ways, but commenced to teach that gentle thing to fight by butting with its head, though as it came to pass most luckily, the cat came to a place where its mischief was stopped, as you shall hear soon, so that señor sheep was left with his lesson half or less than half learned, so that the youngest child now need not fear a whole flock.

But for the most part the cat slept in the daytime, so did not make all the mischief that she might have made, although she dreamed mischief, let it be remembered. But this

was the bad thing of it: her dream came to life and walked
the earth in the shape of a man with a fox face, and a very
terrible monster was he, for being a dream man he could not
be killed. That you may see for yourself.

Sometimes he appeared among men, dressed in fine robes
in a way of a rich man, clothes wonderfully fine, as fine as
those that you may see about the men pictured on the playing cards. Sometimes it was otherwise and he came as one
all worn and travel-stained. Sometimes he came as a head
without a body, making mouths or looking slantwise; sometimes he ran at people, did this dream man, ran with hooked
fingers and claw nails and made it so that the one he chased
could not run at all, or running, moved but slowly. For such
must be the nature of the dreams of cats, as everyone knows
who has seen a cat with a mouse. But whichever way the
dream man came, mischief of some kind walked with him,
and for the most part he did his evil work by granting men
their wishes. For you must know that no man knows the
thing that is best for him and for his welfare, and many are
apt to see some little things as desirable, the which in time
work out for their own undoing. Thus, once there was a man
who was a woodcutter, and growing weary of hard work he
sat him down under a tree and sighed, saying that though
he worked hard, yet his work was never done, and there were
many mouths to feed. Then who should appear before him
but the fox-faced man, which of course was but the cat-
dream come to life, the cat meantime being asleep in the sun.
So this happened:

"Why do you complain?" asked the fox-faced one, who
knew very well what was afoot.

"All day I cut and chop, and chop and cut, but at the end
of the day little is the work that I have done, and my very

children for whom I toil, and for whom my wife toils, do but grumble that I am not rich," answered the poor fellow, who was indeed a very worthy man.

"Lucky for you, then, is it that you have seen me," said fox-face. "For know that I have it in my power to grant you a wish. What then would you have?"

Hearing that, the woodcutter was thoughtful, for, in the manner of those who see a dream man, everything seemed right and proper. Still, while he had in his life wished for many things from day to day, when the time came to make a wish he had none ready. Then his eye fell on his ax and he said without thinking: "For one thing I wish that my ax was an ax so that when I cut a stick or anything, I would have two as big as the first one."

To be sure, had he given thought he might have seen how foolish a wish was that, as both cat and fox-face knew. But he spoke as the wind blew. Then fox-face said some words which the woodcutter did not understand, and added: "Try now your ax."

So the man took a stick about the size of a man's arm and brought down his ax in the middle of it, and lo, there were two sticks, each the size of a man's arm, instead of two pieces each the half of that. The man looked up, open-mouthed and surprised, to say something, but fox-face had vanished, for the cat had wakened and so her dream ceased.

But greatly amazed was the man, for, as he soon saw, all his chopping was of no account, for a tree cut down became at once two trees and one of those trees cut in halves became two trees again. As for cutting smaller wood, that, too, soon became impossible, seeing that each stick grew to two sticks, so that soon he had to cease work because of the wood all about him. Worse still, as he went to the place where he lived, there came across his path a poisonous serpent, and forgetting for a moment the power of his ax he cut the snake in two, and there, hissing before him, were two snakes. So he fled to his people and told them the tale, at which they wondered greatly. But to make sure that the ax would do no mischief, and in truth somewhat fearing it, they hung it in a tree, and each man told his son the story of it, so that all might come to know it as a thing best left alone.

II

Now in the course of time there came to that place a very wise man who had seen many wonders. It had come to his ears that the cat was a creature of darkness, teaching harmless things evil tricks, but of the fox-faced man he knew nothing. The cat only, he considered. So the wise man walked the mountains for many days, and one day when the sky was low and it was a day of rain, an unpleasant day for the cat, he came upon the evil-minded creature hurrying somewhere.

"Why in so great a hurry?" asked the wise man. "Sit awhile with me and talk."

"No. No," said the cat. "I like not your water and I seek a place where there is shelter, so that I may be dry and warm." Indeed, the cat looked very miserable indeed.

"Well, how would you like to have a house of stone?" asked the wise man.

"That I should like very much indeed," answered the cat. "But it must be a house large enough for me, and with no room for any other creature, for I am not fond of company. But a house in which I could sit and dream, and where no noises might disturb, would be very pleasant. Make me such a one and I shall teach you something. Or how about a wish?

Would you like to have claws like an owl? Or would you like to drink blood like a vampire bat? Or would you like to spit poison? Or would you like to bristle like a porcupine?"

"Thank you, no," said the wise man. "I want nothing. But by to-morrow there shall be a house ready for you."

"Where is it to be built?" asked the cat. "First, it must be in a quiet place where men do not go."

"It shall be that," answered the wise man. "But just now I do not know where the place may be. I must seek a proper place."

"Then how shall I find it?" asked the cat.

"Attend," said the wise man. "I shall put a thread about the world, a thread that no man may break with his hands, and when you see that thread, follow it and so come to the stone house."

"Agreed," said the cat. "But let the house be just big enough for me. Let it be in a quiet place. Also, let it be of such fashion that I can slip out backward or leap out forward should an enemy come."

So that being said and no more to come, man and cat parted.

But mark well what followed. On the next day the cat chanced to see the thread and followed it, walking down hill and up hill, down mountain and up mountain, until she arrived at a high place where stood the wise man. At his feet were three flat stones, two standing upright, the third across the top of the two, so that it was like two sides of a little house, roofed and of a comforable size for the cat. So after looking about carefully and suspiciously, the cat entered into it and coiled her tail about her, blinked her eyes once, twice, thrice, then slept. And as soon as she was well asleep the wise man fastened the thread about her neck, the same thread which went about the world and which no man could break with his hands, there being magic about it, and señora cat was bound for years, and would have been bound for ever, had it not been for Nasca, about whom you shall hear.

That ends the tale of the cat, though there is much more to come. And if you are in a hurry to get to the rest of the tale, you may skip from this—to the three stars * * * again, without losing much.

I said that it ended the tale of the cat, but it does not. It ends the first part only, for Adolpho went only thus far, and the telling took the whole of an evening, for there was much looping and winding in his telling and he added much that had nothing to do with the tale. Indeed, you should be very grateful indeed to me for trimming all the uninteresting stuff away. And let me tell you this: it was not at all easy to get Adolpho to tell the rest of the tale, and the place in which we sat when we talked was not comfortable. It was no house with radiators and electric lights, or bathtubs and bookshelves. Indeed, the only furniture that we had was a frying-pan without a handle and an iron pot. As for our house, it looked more like a short stout bottle than a dwelling. For the truth is that we were careless builders and had made our house out of sods of earth; but while we started to build a square house, we did not take care of the corners, and the house came roundish and the walls leaned inward as they went higher, so we left the top open by way of chimney, for our fire was built in the middle of the floor. Thus such was the shape of our house that we had to sleep curved and we had to stand curved, though we rarely stood, because of the smoke, I assure you.

Almost three weeks passed away before Adolpho told me the rest of the tale and it was a cold night in June when he did. After supper he commenced, perhaps because it was the kind of stew that he liked best. For the most of the stew was fish. I said "the most of the stew," because our stews were different from those you have. If on Monday we had a piece of huanaco meat, we put it in the iron pot to stew. There would be something left over, for we always made a little more than we required and we never wasted food. So, supper being done, the iron pot with the remains of the stew was put aside. Perhaps next day we might have caught or shot a young goose, or something like that. Anyway, whatever we caught went into the pot by way of stew. So that day there would be goose stew with a flavour of huanaco. Next day we might add charqui, which is dried horse-flesh, to the stew, so while the chief thing would be charqui, there would be a decided flavour of goose and more than a trace of huanaco. But if we had fish on the fourth day, then of course it would be strongly fishy stew, with a kind of side taste of charqui, a flavour of goose, and a mild trace of huanaco. On the whole it was satisfactory, for toward the end of the week any one might find something to his liking, though on Saturday we always cleaned out the pot, as we needed it for our week's washing. And so, as I say, when we came one evening to fish stew, Adolpho was in high good humour and told me the rest of the tale, and this is how his story ran.

*   *   *

The Second Part of the Tale

Now, began Soto, you must remember all that I have told you about the cat bound on the mountain top, the magic ax hanging in the tree, and the hundreds and hundreds of years that passed, with the cat growing larger and larger. As the cat grew, so did the house, for the wise man had promised that it should be just big enough for the cat, and he kept his word. But you must also remember that the cat could not move, but could certainly dream. So she dreamed of many lands, and the dream man was very active indeed, though he vanished whenever the cat woke.

When you come to think of it, you will see that it was a most excellent thing that the cat was bound, for had she not been, she would have worked her mischief on the world and a sheep might have been as terrible as a wild boar or flies as annoying as mosquitoes or horses as bold as wild bulls or the very fish as poisonous as serpents. While the cat did not dream, of course the fox-faced man was nowhere, and then all went very well and trees put out their blossoms and fruits, the grass was softly green, the rain was like silver, and gentle were the hearts of men as they went about their affairs.

But there was a day on which the cat dreamed and the fox-faced fellow was busy. To the place where lived the people who guarded the magic ax, there came a stranger. His eyes were aslant and little, the hair of him was reddish, and he was in rags and tatters and altogether dirty in appearance. To be sure, no one would look twice at rags and tatters, for one coming through the forest must needs be torn by thorns and bushes in all that tangle, but dirt was quite another matter, especially when the dirt included blood stains, because in that place was much water and many running streams, nor was the water chill to the skin. So, because of the uncleanness of the man, people looked at him with unfriendly eyes, and though they were neither insolent nor rude they hoped that he would go farther and not stay there. Nor would it have been any great hardship for him to do so, seeing that it was a place of much fruit and of many berries, and roots pleasant to the taste and full of nourishment. As for the night, any man might well stretch himself under that star-sprinkled sky, nor except for the beasts that the cat had made unfriendly were there creatures to do harm. But the stranger had no notion of doing anything to please the people, nor indeed could he do anything, seeing that he was the creature of the cat's dream, walking the world.

For a time then he stood under a tree bewailing his lot and crying out that all the world was against him and saying that none were kind to him. Strange things he did, too, as is the manner of dream people, making himself sometimes shoot far far away so that he looked small, then coming near again and getting big, or sometimes pointing his finger at someone, then throwing his arm round and round in great circles, the finger always pointing, the circles he made growing smaller and smaller, little by little, but his finger always pointing, until it came close to the watcher's eyes. The people thought this an annoying thing for a stranger to do; but so it was. And always he woefully wailed. So those there stood about him in a little circle, none going close, but all wondering much at the great outcry, the like of which none there had heard before. Then he began to sing, noisily, wildly. This was his song:

> "Over the world I walk,
>   Alone, for ever alone.
> Trouble and trial and care,
>   Alone, I bear alone.
> Torture and pain I bear,
>   Alone, for ever alone.
> Wandering day and night,

> Alone, for ever alone.
> Sad and wretched my plight,
> Alone, for ever alone."

Then he gave a long, long cry, like a wolf:

> "A—a—a—a—a——lone, Oo—oo—oo—oo!"

Nor did he stop at that, for his song done, he began to act stupidly, leaping from side to side in rage and fury, mouthing and grimacing, opening and closing his fists, but making no noise. Then he talked again, but it was a jabber of idle words, so presently those about him shook their heads at one another, looking at him as one who had lost his wits, never thinking of course that he was a cat's dream.

While all this was going on, there came from the little lake where he had been fishing a lad named Nasca, bearing a basket of fish, a happy fellow who always made music and song as he walked, and seeing the people gathered about the stranger he drew near. No sooner did the stranger clap eyes on the fish than he leaped at the basket and began devouring the silvery things, eating them raw, heads, bodies, and tails, for thus ran the cat's dream and cattishness must out. But the meal being done, the stranger redoubled his lamentations, all the time swinging his arm in circles, sometimes great, sometimes small, with his finger pointed at the boy.

"A—a—a—a—a——lone, Oo—oo—oo—oo!" he screamed, and the boy thought that such a fellow well deserved to be alone, but he was too polite to say so.

"I am hungry and travel-worn," the stranger went on. "Is there no one here who will give me shelter? Is there no one in this place with a kind heart to pity me?"

Hearing that, the heart of Nasca was touched, for never had he, nor never had his grandmother with whom he lived,

turned a hungry creature away empty. Indeed, so gentle in
spirit was Nasca that if the stem of a flower was broken by
a heedless creature he was full of grief. Yet the doings of
the stranger astonished him and troubled him, for the man
without seeming to move his feet thrust his face close to the
boy's, then somehow took his face far off. That silly trick he
did again and again as dream creatures do, so that seeing him
Nasca was well nigh made dizzy. Then the lad, blushing
red as fire because of all the people thereabouts who did not
offer what he offered, said:

"Come home, then, with me. Our house is small but there
is room enough. Believe me, it is not that these people are
hard-hearted that they do not seem to welcome you, but more
because you must have been too weary with walking to wash
yourself. But behind the hill and under a tree near where
we live is a still pool, and there doubtless you will clean
yourself."

Then Nasca led the way and the stranger went with him,
yet not walking, but leaping up and down as he went, and
sometimes not touching the ground at all. Nasca was not
comfortable with the stranger by his side, for he felt him to
be more like a shadow than a man, and a shadow that hung
over him and tormented him, a shadow that might pounce
upon him.

Having come to the place where his grandmother was,
Nasca was sorely troubled to see the old woman fall to trembling when she heard the voice of the stranger, who was
making an idle jabber of words again. Indeed, after a time
she put her hands to her face and wept, though that was
after the man having eaten had left the place to rest under
a tree. Nasca comforted her as best he could, then asked
her to tell him the cause of her grief. Be it remembered that

she was very, very old and her eyes were weak and dim with age.

"Tell me," she said, taking Nasca's hand, "has this man eyes aslant, like the eyes of a fox?"

"Indeed and he has," answered Nasca. Then his heart bade him say some good of the fellow, and he added: "Yet no man makes his own face, wherefore must some be pitied."

"Tell me," said the grandmother eagerly, "has he sharp teeth like a cat?"

"That he has," said Nasca, then wondering, asked: "Have you seen this man, then, when your eyes were bright and strong?"

"No, Nasca," she answered, "never have I set eyes on him, yet I greatly fear him; and long, long ago I heard stories about such a creature and it was said that much evil he wrought, yet none could slay him." She was silent for a little, then again she asked this: "Did you see his ears, Nasca, and are they pointed, like those of a fox?"

"Yes," said Nasca.

At that answer the old woman was sad again and Nasca had to comfort her with sweet words, telling her that she should come to no hurt, since he was there, for he would die defending her.

"That I know, Nasca," she said. "If the hurt came to me alone, glad would I be, for I have seen my golden days and now there is little left for me but the brief sunset hour. But I fear for others. Of such a creature I have heard it said that he comes from nowhere and goes into nothing, but somehow looses evil upon men. Because of that I fear. So, Nasca, promise me that if this man asks anything of you, you will do nothing that promises hurt to any living thing."

That Nasca promised gladly enough, then said: "Yet it

may be that this man is not the evil creature you have heard of. It may well be some unfortunate whose wits are loose. True, his face is far from pleasant to see, but a rough face may go with a good heart, and a man's face may change."

"Yes, with wickedness," said the old woman, "but in truth it has been said that a man's face and his character both go with him to the grave, if indeed there is any grave for such as this."

II

Now all that talk Nasca remembered well the next day when a strange thing happened. For the stranger went about among the people, asking this one and that what he most desired. But there were none to make a wish for a time, because life there was pleasant and easy and the possessions of men were few, so all that the stranger said went for nothing. Then, as it chanced, there came one of the people a little put out because he had lost sleep that morning. He was a man much given to rest and slumber, a slow and heavy man, and that morning he had been awakened by the singing of the birds. To make matters worse, going away from the place where he had lain, in too great a hurry, he chanced to scratch himself on some thorns. So, taking it all in all, his humour was not a pleasant one; yet had it not been for the stranger, he might have forgotten his troubles. As it was, he heard the stranger's speech and the offer to grant any wish, so he spoke without considering his words.

"If you grant wishes, there is one that I would have," he said, nodding to his friends in the manner of one who had a matter of weight to tell of.

"Say it," said the stranger, and he grinned queerly so that his lip went up and his tusky teeth shone yellow.

"This morning I was disturbed by birds and scratched by thorns, so I wish that nothing might come near me to disturb me in the future."

"As you wish," said the stranger, and gabbled what seemed to be idle and meaningless words.

Then a strange thing happened, for as the man who had made the wish stood looking at the stranger, his mouth wide open, all living things about him suddenly fell away. Within the stretch of a man's arm from him the grass yellowed and died, and the flowers shrank and withered, and a butterfly that fluttered over him fell to earth, dead. And the people cried out, seeing that, but soon it became clear that not even sounds could come within that magic circle. The air bore no noise to the charmed man, not even the sweet noise of the songs of birds nor the chirping of insects, and the man was, in very truth, in such case that nothing could be nigh him to disturb him. Indeed, as he moved, all things died within the stretch of his arms, seeing which his friends fled from him, all fearful of his nearness. Afraid of his loneliness the man walked to a tree, but no sooner did he touch it than the very leaves folded themselves and turned black, then dropped off and fluttered down, so that the arms of the good tree stood skeleton-bare against the sky. At that all hope in the man was gone and he turned and fled into the forest, a space opening before him as he ran, a track of death everywhere behind him.

Nasca saw all that, and his grandmother's fears came to his mind. Indeed, he told many there of what the old woman had said, but some of them held that the stranger had but granted the wisher his wish, and if there was fault in the matter the fault lay with the wisher, not with the granter of the wish. As for the grandmother, when she heard the tale she was in great trouble and threw herself on the ground weeping, and though Nasca did what he could to comfort her, yet she wept and wept.

"Nasca," she said presently, "surely we must do what we can to rid the place of this fearful creature. For it is as I thought, and he is a black-hearted thing, not of this world of men, and one who will assuredly bring hate and fear and trouble. Find, then, if there is any means by which he may be made to go away, even to the point of helping him, if need be, but see to it that you think not of yourself and your own gain, and see to it that anything that you do at his request will bring no harm to any living creature, even the smallest."

All this Nasca promised, and in the early dawn of the next day went up to the hills to see the sun rise, as indeed did all brave and strong men and fair maidens in that place. Then he swam a little while, and ate some fruit and thought a while, and after sought out the stranger.

"Stranger," said he, "be it known to you that there are many here who fear your presence among us and who would be glad to see you gone from here."

"Ho! Ho! What bold words are these I hear?" roared fox-face, full of wrath at Nasca's words.

"I speak but the truth," said the lad boldly enough, though his heart beat against his ribs. "Tell me, then, what can be done so that you may be persuaded to leave us."

Fox-face thought awhile, then he said: "On a far mountain is a gentle creature bound with a magic thread which no man's hand can break. Yet magic fights magic, and the magic ax can sever the thread. Also, at the moment the thread is cut, so will the man who is prisoned in air be free, but not before. Now the bound creature is my companion and no fierce thing at all. Come with me, Nasca, bringing the magic ax, and when you have seen the cat, then perchance shall the spell be broken."

All of that seeming fair to Nasca, he went to the tree where hung the magic ax, though he had much ado to climb through the tangle all about the tree, for no man had been there for many a year. He took the ax and fastened it well in his sash, and returned to the side of the stranger. Then fox-face took a mat made of feathers of the night owl and the hair of the skunk, and spread it on the ground, but it was so small that there was scarce place for Nasca and the man too, so the lad cut it with the magic ax and there were two mats, which was more to Nasca's taste, for he had no liking to stand on the mat and hold on to fox-face. No sooner had they taken their places on the mats than they rose in the air, and in a swift moment both of them were so high that the country lay spread at their feet with trees like grass and with rivers that looked like silver threads. Nor could the swiftest condor move with the speed with which they flew through the air. So at last they came to a place where everywhere were bare rocks and hard stone, with no blade of grass to be seen, and it was a place among mountain peaks, with stony ridge rising above stony ridge, and on a mountain peak the two rested.

"Now look away to the far hill," said the stranger, and while the place to which he pointed was very far off, yet because of the clearness of the air it seemed but a short distance away. Looking steadily Nasca saw the three great rocks, for they were tremendously grown now, after so many hundreds of years, but to Nasca they seemed no higher than a man's knee, and sitting under them was the cat.

"That is the companion I seek," said fox-face. "By magic

she is bound and by magic only can she be loosed, and I promise you that if you will but loose her I shall be seen no more in your land."

"Fair enough," said Nasca. "But I must be assured of a return to my own place, for it is far from home on these hills."

"That is well enough," answered fox-face. "Have you not your flying mat? Though to be sure, as soon as you take your foot from it it will vanish."

Nasca thought for a little while, and the more he thought the more it seemed to him to be a good thing and not an evil to loose the cat, so he asked the stranger to show him the bond that held her. At that fox-face pointed, and there almost at his feet Nasca beheld a slender thread, like a hair, that ran this way and that as far as the eye could see. So with a blow of the magic ax he cut the thread, and there was a noise like thunder and the thread ends slid away like swift snakes. Nor did the stranger play Nasca false, for in a flash he found himself back again at the foot of the tree where the magic ax had hung, and so swiftly had the journey been made that a man who had stooped to fill his calabash at a pool when Nasca left, was even then straightening himself to go away, his calabash being filled. As for the fox-faced stranger, no one ever saw him again, for the cat being awakened, her dream had ended. And at the moment when the thread was cut, the man who had been bound in air came back again, his enchantment finished, and the things that had died about him, because of invisible forces, sprang to life again.

But what of the cat? For Nasca little thought that he had loosed a fearful thing on the world, a frightful form of giant mould of a size bigger than a bull. Nor did he know until one evening, as he sat by the fire, it being chill in that high place at times, he turned his head as the robe that hung at the door bulged into the house. He looked to see his grandmother, but instead a great cat filled the doorway, a cat with green eyes, each the size of an egg. Indeed so great was the cat that it had to crouch low to enter. And when within, the room was filled with it, a sight that made the heart of Nasca stand still. A gloomy terror it was, and most fiendish was the look that it gave the lad. But Nasca, though terror-stricken, yet showed no sign of fear. Instead, he made room for the cat by the fire as though he saw cats like that every day. So the cat sat by the fire and close to Nasca, sometimes looking at the blaze without winking, sometimes turning its great head to look for long and long at the boy. Once Nasca stood up, saying that he would go outside and bring in more wood for the fire, privately thinking to get out of the place in safety, but the great paw of the cat shot out with claws that looked like reaping hooks, whereupon Nasca sat down again saying that, after all, the fire would live awhile. But he thought and thought and the cat looked and looked, and the place was as still and quiet as a midnight pool.

Presently Nasca found heart to say something.

"If you want to stay here and rest," he said to the cat, "I shall go away."

"You must not go away," said the cat in a soft voice, stretching out one of her paws with the cruel claws showing a little.

After that a long time passed and the fire flamed only a little, and the shadow of the cat was big and black on the wall, and Nasca thought and thought and the cat looked and looked. Then the firelight danced and the big black shadow seemed to leap and then grow small, and the cat's eyes were full of a cold fire as they rested on Nasca.

Then suddenly Nasca broke into a laugh, though, to be sure, the laugh did not come from his heart.

"Why do you laugh?" said the cat.

"Because you are so big and I am so little, but for all that I can run ten times faster than you," answered Nasca, and his words sounded bold enough. He added: "All living creatures would agree in that."

"That is nonsense," said the cat, her jealousy at once aroused. "I am the fastest creature on earth. I can leap over mountains and I take rivers at a step."

"It does not matter what you can do," said Nasca, growing bolder every second. "Let me tell you this: While a man stooped to fill his calabash, I went from this place to a far mountain, cut the thread that bound you, and returned before the man with the calabash had straightened himself, and if you do not believe it, I will bring the man."

Nasca said all this with some idea of getting an excuse to go from there, but the words struck deep and the cat wondered.

"Why did you loose me?" asked the cat.

"Because I wanted to run a race with you," answered Nasca.

"If we run a race it must be for a wager," said the cat. "If you lose I make a meal of you. Is it agreed?"

"Fairly spoken," said Nasca, "though to be sure if you lose I make no meal of you."

"Let us run to-morrow then," said Nasca. "And I shall sleep well under the tree and be fresh in the morning."

"Not so," said the cat. "If we run, we run at midnight and under the cold white moon."

"So be it," answered Nasca. "Where shall we run?"

"Across the mountains and back again, seven times," said the cat, choosing the highlands, because she knew that she could leap over hills and cañons, while Nasca would have to climb up and down, and choosing night because she could see better in the dark than Nasca. For the cat was very wise. But Nasca on his part thought of little more than getting away from the cat for a while. So he told the cat that he would bring a basket of fish for her supper, which he did, and while the cat ate he went outside and sought his grandmother.

The wise old woman laughed when she heard the story. "To a cat her cattishness," she said, "but to a woman her wit. All falls out well enough. Haste, run and bring me the magic ax."

"But no," said Nasca. "To use that would but make two terrible cats, and one is more than enough."

"Heed me, Nasca, and bring the ax," she repeated.

At that the boy ran swiftly and brought the ax.

"Now stand, Nasca, and fear not," said the old woman, and lifted the ax. So the lad stood, closing his eyes when he saw her raise the ax to strike.

Then with a swift blow she brought the weapon down on Nasca's head, cutting him in two, and in a moment there stood before her two Nascas, each as like the other as one blade of grass is like another. Surely and well had the ax done its work. One Nasca was as shapely as the other, one as fair-skinned as the other.

"Now," said the old woman, "happy was I with one Nasca, so doubly happy shall I be with two. So stay you here, Nasca the first, and Nasca the second must come with me. Oh, a merry world and a glad will it be now, since joy and gladness are doubled."

At that she remembered that she had told neither lad anything, in her delight, so she turned again to the first Nasca.

"Wait here for the great cat," she said. "Go with her to the great cañon where the race must start, and when the cat makes to leap across, which she will do, do you climb down a little way, then hide yourself until the cat returns. Doubtless we shall be able to manage matters at the other end. But see to it that you chide the cat for her slowness when she returns after the first run, and we shall see what we shall see."

Having said that, the old woman set off with Nasca the second, walking bravely over the ridges and hills that rose one behind the other like the waves of the sea. And when they had come to a far place where the mountain dropped down like a great stone wall to a fearful depth, they sat them down to wait, Nasca the second being in plain sight, the old woman hiding behind a rock.

But as soon as the moon rose the great cat walked to where Nasca the first stood, her eyes glaring terribly and her hair all a-bristle. So horrible a sight was she that for a moment Nasca went deadly pale, but he spoke boldly enough, nevertheless, for the brave one is not he that does not fear, but rather he that fears and yet does the thing that he has set out to do.

"One thing," said Nasca to the cat. "Is it right that you should leap over the cañon, going from one side to the other like a bird, while I must climb down and then up again? Let us make things fairer in the race, and do you climb down and up the other side with me." But all this he said in a kind

of spirit of mischief, knowing full well that the cat would
give him no chance at all.

"Ha! What is to do now?" said the cat with a hiss and
a sneer. "Does your heart fail you already? Are you terror-
tormented at the start? A fine racer, you, indeed! No, no, my
fine lad. We race for a supper and you must supply the
meal."

To that Nasca answered nothing, so there was a little
silence, broken only by the hooting of the owl who was, indeed, trying to tell the cat the truth of matters. But the cat
was too full of her own notions and had no ear for others.
She lay crouched on the ground, ready to make a spring,
and Nasca wondered whether her jump would be at him or
across the cañon. Suddenly, in a voice like thunder, the cat
called: "START!" and at the word, leaped across the valley
and was off and away, without as much as giving a glance
at the lad. But he made a great deal of fuss on his part,
climbing down the face of the cañon wall. The cat, on land-
ing on the other side, looked back, then gave a cry of tri-
umph, seeing the poor start that Nasca had made. "Come on!
Come on!" she called. "The run will sharpen my appetite,"
and even as she said that, she was a distance off, then bounding away up hill and down hill, over the ridges, over the
rocks, over the streams, taking a hundred yards at a bound.
So in a very short space of time she came to the place where
Nasca the second stood, and was mightily astonished to see
her opponent, as she thought, there before her.

"Too easy, señora cat, too easy," said Nasca the second,
speaking as the grandmother bade him. "I thought cats were
swifter. Doubtless you play, though."

Hearing that speech the cat was full of anger and in a

voice that shook the mountains, she roared: "BACK! BACK AGAIN! I'll show you."

Off ran Nasca the second then, but the cat passed him like lightning, her very whiskers streaming behind, and as soon as she was over the first hill the lad went back to the place where his grandmother was. Señora cat knew nothing of that, though, and went bounding as before, tearing up hill and down hill, over the ridges, over the rocks, over the streams, taking two hundred yards at a leap, and at last came to the place of beginning, to behold Nasca, who stood smiling and wiping his brow lightly, as if he had been running.

"Much better, señora cat," he said. "You almost caught me that time. A little faster and you would have won. But still I have more speed in me to let loose. Come on."

No sooner were the words out of his mouth than he started off, making as though to climb down the cañon wall, and the cat gave a screech that shook the very skies and made the pale moon quiver. So fast she went that the very trees and bushes that she passed were scorched, and as for the rocks over which she flew, they were melted by the heat of the air. Every leap that she took was four hundred yards. Up hill and down hill she went, over the ridges, over the rocks, over the streams, and so at last she came once more to where the second Nasca stood.

"A good run that, señora cat," he said. "I think that we shall finish the race soon and in a way that I may live and be happy, though for me you must go supperless. Certainly I must try, for to lose will profit me nothing."

But the cat was at her wits' end, supposing that Nasca ran faster than she. She opened her mouth to shriek, but fast upon her came a great feebleness, and she faltered and reeled and then fell down in a faint, seeing nothing at all. No time then did the second Nasca and the old woman lose. Putting themselves to the task, they rolled the cat to the edge of the great rock wall that ran down straight. Then after a pause to gain breath they gave another push, and the body of the giant cat fell over the edge and was broken to pieces on the sharp rocks below. So that was the end of the cat and the end of her dreams.

The two Nascas and the old woman went to their own place and told the people all that had happened, so there was great rejoicing, and laughter and song and weaving of garlands, and everybody was happy. And ever since there has been kindness and good fellowship in that land. And for those who would see signs of the tale there stand the three great rocks on the highlands, each so heavy that two hundred men could not lift them, and wise men wonder much what manner of men put them there. But only those who are not wise and learned know the truth of the matter, as you may test for yourself by asking any very wise men who come to visit you.